PRAISE FOR DONNA GRANT'S
BEST-SELLING ROMANCE NOVELS

"Grant's ability to quickly convey complicated
backstory makes this jam-packed love story accessible
even to new or periodic readers."
—*Publishers' Weekly*

"Donna Grant has given the paranormal genre
a burst of fresh air…"
—*San Francisco Book Review*

"The premise is dramatic and heartbreaking; the characters are
colorful and engaging; the romance is spirited and seductive."
—*The Reading Cafe*

"The central romance, fueled by a hostage drama, plays
out in glorious detail against a backdrop of multiple ongoing
issues in the "Dark Kings" books. This seemingly penultimate
installment creates a nice segue to a climactic end."
—*Library Journal*

"…intense romance amid the growing
war between the Dragons and the
Dark Fae is scorching hot."
—*Booklist*

DRAGON KINGS® SERIES

Dragon Revealed ~ Dragon Mine

Dragon Unbound ~ Dragon Eternal

Dragon Lover ~ Dragon Arisen

Dragon Frost ~ Dragon Kiss ~ Dragon Born

Dragon Marked ~ Dragon Forged ~ Dragon Sieged

SKYE DRUIDS SERIES

Iron Ember ~ Shoulder the Skye ~ Heart of Glass

Endless Skye ~ Still of the Night ~ Blood Skye

After Midnight ~ Kiss of Skye

DARK KINGS SERIES

Dark Heat ~ Darkest Flame ~ Fire Rising

Burning Desire ~ Hot Blooded ~ Night's Blaze

Soul Scorched ~ Dragon King ~ Passion Ignites

Smoldering Hunger ~ Smoke and Fire

Dragon Fever ~ Firestorm ~ Blaze ~ Dragon Burn

Constantine: A History, Parts 1-3 ~ Heat ~ Torched

Dragon Night ~ Dragonfire ~ Dragon Claimed

Ignite ~ Fever ~ Dragon Lost ~ Flame ~ Inferno

A Dragon's Tale (Whisky and Wishes: *A Holiday Novella*,

Heart of Gold: *A Valentine's Novella*, and

Of Fire and Flame) ~ My Fiery Valentine

The Dragon King Coloring Book

Dragon King Special Edition

Character Coloring Book: Rhi

DARK WARRIORS SERIES
Midnight's Master ~ Midnight's Lover
Midnight's Seduction ~ Midnight's Warrior
Midnight's Kiss ~ Midnight's Captive
Midnight's Temptation ~ Midnight's Promise
Midnight's Surrender ~ A Warrior for Christmas

CHIASSON SERIES
Wild Fever ~ Wild Dream ~ Wild Need
Wild Flame ~ Wild Rapture

LARUE SERIES
Moon Kissed ~ Moon Thrall
Moon Struck ~ Moon Bound

WICKED TREASURES
Seized by Passion ~ Enticed by Ecstasy ~ Captured by Desire

✦

HISTORICAL PARANORMAL

THE KINDRED SERIES
Everkin ~ Eversong ~ Everwylde
Everbound ~ Evernight ~ Everspell

KINDRED: THE FATED SERIES
Rage ~ Ruin ~ Reign

DARK SWORD SERIES

Dangerous Highlander

Forbidden Highlander ~ Wicked Highlander

Untamed Highlander ~ Shadow Highlander

Darkest Highlander

ROGUES OF SCOTLAND SERIES

The Craving ~ The Hunger

The Tempted ~ The Seduced

THE SHIELDS SERIES

A Dark Guardian ~ A Kind of Magic

A Dark Seduction ~ A Forbidden Temptation ~ A Warrior's Heart

Mystic Trinity (a series connecting novel)

DRUIDS GLEN SERIES

Highland Mist ~ Highland Nights ~ Highland Dawn

Highland Fires ~ Highland Magic

Mystic Trinity (a series connecting novel)

SISTERS OF MAGIC TRILOGY

Shadow Magic ~ Echoes of Magic ~ Dangerous Magic

THE ROYAL CHRONICLES
NOVELLA SERIES

Prince of Desire ~ Prince of Seduction

Prince of Love ~ Prince of Passion

Mystic Trinity

(a series connecting novel)

Dark Alpha's Redemption

NEW YORK TIMES & USA TODAY BESTSELLING AUTHOR

Donna Grant

www.DonnaGrant.com
www.MotherofDragonsBooks.com

Dark Alpha's Redemption

THE REAPERS

The seven there are, warriors all.
Do not do wrong or their blade will fall.
Their appearances shrouded.
Their approach, clouded.
Against evil they fight.
Power and magic are their might.
They serve only one.
If you expose their identity – run.
Secrecy is their defense.
If the truth escapes, Death will commence.

CHAPTER

one

May

So much had changed. The world as he knew it was entirely different.

And yet, it all felt right.

Bradach stood atop the mountain and looked over the vibrant, colorful realm that Death had created. The tall trees, the deep lakes, the mountains reaching high to the cloudless blue sky.

His new home. Actually, it was home to all Reapers now.

He grinned and shook his head. Their enemy had been vanquished. Bran was no longer a threat. Bradach hated to admit it, but there had been a few times that it felt as if Bran would win. But the Reapers had succeeded in defeating their foe.

Bradach's gaze slid to the left. In the distance nestled in a valley, he was able to make out the top of the white tower, Death's home.

Well, hers and Cael's now.

Maybe it was because Bradach was in the second group of Reapers, but he hadn't had a clue that there was something between Erith and Cael. The fact that Cael's Reapers, as well as Bradach's leader, Eoghan, were pleased about it, said that most had taken notice of something during their long eons together.

Bradach was happy for the couple. Though he wasn't sure what was going to become of Cael's group since he was . . . more . . . now. The battle with Bran had changed Cael. Bran had syphoned some of Death's powers and then used them on Cael.

And as only Cael could, he'd managed to harness the poisonous magic running through him and let it meld with his own. The act not only changed his eyes from silver to dark purple, but he was also now as powerful as Death herself.

It made Erith and Cael a couple that no one should ever think to cross.

Bradach drew in a deep breath and slowly released it. As he did, he spotted an approaching figure. The moment Eoghan cleared the tree line, Bradach smiled in greeting.

Eoghan came to stand beside him and let his gaze wander over the terrain. "What a magnificent view."

"There isn't a place on this realm that isn't stunning," Bradach agreed. "From the mountains to the deserts to the forests to the vast oceans."

"I would expect nothing less from Erith."

Bradach folded his arms over his chest. He and the other five Reapers of Eoghan's group had been rotating in shifts to look for Xaneth. The royal Light Fae had disappeared during the battle with Bran, and they had yet to find him.

Xaneth had joined Death in the fight against Bran, but the fact that the Queen of the Light, Usaeil, wanted Xaneth dead, made her the prime suspect in his vanishing. It didn't help that no one had seen Usaeil in weeks.

"Is it time?" Bradach asked.

Eoghan turned his head of long, black hair to Bradach, the leader's liquid silver gaze meeting Bradach's. Few things unnerved him, but Eoghan's eyes were one of them. They had been altered after a trip to another realm. Now, there were no pupils in Eoghan's eyes. Just pools of silver.

"Our hunt for Xaneth hasn't paid off. We've searched Ireland dozens of times, as well as the rest of Earth. Neither Usaeil nor Xaneth is anywhere to be found," Eoghan stated.

Bradach pressed his lips together briefly. This is what they had all feared. It didn't bode well that not even Erith could locate Usaeil. "There are two places we've not looked."

Eoghan held Bradach's gaze for a long moment. "You mean the Dark Palace and the Light Castle."

"Aye."

"Balladyn is also searching for Xaneth. For whatever reason, the King of the Dark has an affinity for the royal."

"And you believe what he says?" Bradach asked, not even trying to hide his disbelief—or his disapproval. Then again, all things Dark Fae set him on edge.

One side of Eoghan's mouth lifted in a grin. "If Usaeil hadn't betrayed Balladyn, you would've grown up worshiping him as one of the greatest generals in the Light army."

"Instead, he's now King of the Dark."

"He's a survivor," Eoghan replied, a hard edge to his voice. "He was betrayed, just like every Reaper. The darkness hasn't stolen all of his light. It's still there. The proof is in his affiliation with Xaneth, as well as when Balladyn joined us to fight Bran."

Bradach could point out that the King of the Dark had done

that so Bran would stop kidnapping the Dark Fae, but he didn't bother. Eoghan must see something in Balladyn that Bradach didn't. There was no use bickering about it. Bradach had his views about the Dark Fae—and they would never change.

Eoghan made a sound at the back of his throat. "Even after serving as a Reaper with both Dark and Light Fae, you still hold a grudge against the Dark."

There was no use denying it. So, Bradach didn't.

"I see," Eoghan said and looked away. There was disappointment in not only his voice but also in his gaze.

Bradach felt compelled to explain his reasons. "The Reapers are different. We're neither Light nor Dark once we accept Death's offer. We're simply . . . Reapers."

Eoghan sighed heavily. "That's true, of course. But we each still have the coloring of what we were. The proof of how we lived and what side we chose is there for all to see."

As if Bradach needed reminding that Dark Fae had red eyes and silver in their black hair. The more silver, the more evil they had committed.

Eoghan crossed his arms over his chest and looked back at Bradach. "Erith considers Balladyn an ally. That may change, but for the moment, there will most likely be instances when we will need to interact with the King of the Dark."

"Are you asking me if I can do that?" Bradach snorted in annoyance. He really, really hoped that wasn't what Eoghan was doing. Because Bradach hadn't liked Balladyn joining them against Bran, but he hadn't exactly had a say in it.

Eoghan merely stared at him in response.

When Bradach became a Reaper, he'd vowed to follow Death's orders, no matter what they might be. It didn't matter that Eoghan stood beside him now. Every order that came to the Reapers came from Erith herself.

Bradach sighed softly, knowing what he had to say, regardless of how difficult it might be. "I'll do whatever is asked of me. Even if I don't agree with it. Death appointed you our leader, and you won my trust. I thought I made that clear."

Eoghan nodded slowly. "You did. But I know your history. That's what worries me."

Bradach looked away, not wanting to delve into the past. Even Eoghan mentioning it was enough to make him tense up and sink into a rage that was becoming harder and harder to come back from every time he fell into it. It's why he didn't think of his past.

Ever.

"I learned a long time ago never to offer advice if someone doesn't ask," Eoghan said after a moment. "But I'm going to give it to you anyway. Trust me when I tell you that no matter how far you run or how deep you bury those memories you don't want to think about, they'll rise up and consume you when you least expect it. Deal with them. Face your past and put it to rest, once and for all."

It was good counsel. Bradach could admit that, but he still couldn't do as Eoghan suggested. It was too . . . agonizing. He dropped his arms to his sides and squeezed his eyes closed as he guessed where all this talk was leading.

"You're sending me to the Dark Palace." Bradach turned his head to look at Eoghan, waiting for confirmation.

"I am."

"Wouldn't Dubhan, Cathal, or even Aisling be better?"

"Why?" Eoghan questioned, a black brow quirked. "Because they were once Dark?"

Bradach nodded. "Not to put so fine a point on it, but aye."

"Which is exactly why they can't go. They could be recognized, and that isn't something we can chance."

In his head, Bradach was shifting through arguments to change Eoghan's mind when his leader spoke again.

"The simple truth is, we need you in the palace," Eoghan said. "You see everything. It's your skill set, Bradach. Balladyn will see through your glamour, but that doesn't matter since you'll be working with him."

For fek's sake. Could things get any worse? What had he done to piss Eoghan off so that he'd get sent on the one mission he wanted no part of?

There were numerous reasons Bradach could list why one of the other Reapers would be better for the job, but he didn't let a single one pass his lips. When he took Death's offer, he had done it knowing that he was at her mercy. She was his queen now, and by association, Eoghan was his general.

Whatever was asked of him, Bradach would do it. No matter how much he wished otherwise.

"This isn't a punishment," Eoghan said as if reading his mind. "I chose you because of how you see things. We need details. All details, right now. I'm aware that being around the Dark will be difficult for you."

Bradach snorted loudly but kept his response to himself.

Eoghan's lips thinned for a heartbeat. "But I also know you, Bradach. You're a Reaper because Death saw your skills as a warrior. Erith and I both believe you can handle this."

Bradach steeled himself. No doubt this was Death's way of getting him to face his past. She'd only mentioned it once before, but it wasn't a coincidence that Eoghan had said something now. Bradach released a long breath and then said, "Tell me what you want me to do."

"I don't ask this of you lightly," Eoghan stated.

Bradach shrugged, his hands clutched into fists. It had to be done, and he had been chosen. That's all that mattered.

Eoghan gave a bow of his head. "You have the skill set needed to see the mission through. Rordan is too much of a smartass. I need someone cool-headed. Torin would let his pain rule him."

"And you believe I won't."

"No," Eoghan replied. "You won't. You never do. It also helps that others underestimate you."

Bradach issued a bark of laughter. "Because I don't look like a typical warrior."

"Because you don't look like a typical warrior," Eoghan repeated with a grin. "That will work as an advantage if you do have to fight."

"No collecting souls while I'm there?" Bradach asked with a smirk.

Eoghan lifted one shoulder as he smiled. "You never know. Death may pass judgment."

That was unlikely, and they both knew it. The reaping of souls had been taken over by Cael's group for the moment. They'd earned a break after everything they had been through with Bran.

"Is this where you've chosen to make your home?" Eoghan asked to change the subject.

Bradach thought about the life he'd had on the Fae Realm and shook his head. "I came up here for the view, but I won't live on another mountain."

"Have you picked out a location yet?"

Erith had given the entire realm to them, allowing each of the Reapers to choose where they wanted to have a home, though there would be a main building not far from her white tower where they would go for meetings and gatherings. The hidden realm allowed them to live together but apart.

Which was great for Cael's group since each of them had a wife. Another change to the Reapers, but one that Bradach had no issue with. He might not believe in love, but he acknowledged that some people—very few—had a deep connection.

"Bradach?" Eoghan prodded.

He realized then that he hadn't answered Eoghan's question. He lifted one shoulder. "There are a couple of places that have intrigued me. I'll make a decision when this mission is finished. When do I leave?"

"Immediately."

Bradach raised a brow as he waited for Eoghan to continue. "What's my task?"

"Maeve."

Bradach gaped at Eoghan, utterly shocked—and unsure if he'd heard correctly. "Maeve the Merciless? You can't be serious."

"I want you to find out all you can about her and the workings of her business. Balladyn informed us that Maeve and Usaeil were friendly. This could potentially help us locate Xaneth."

"Usaeil doesn't have friends," Bradach pointed out.

"No, she doesn't. But the fact that she trusts Maeve enough to visit her often means that Maeve might know something about the queen we don't."

Bradach sighed loudly. "Even the Light know Maeve. She's ruthless and uncompromising. She destroys anyone who even hints at betraying her. Fierce. Vicious. Brutal."

"She's all that and more," Eoghan said.

"She could have the Dark throne if she wanted it. Well," Bradach said when he thought of Balladyn, "she could have taken it from Taraeth. But the current king is a different animal altogether."

Eoghan grinned, nodding in agreement. "Which is why she has made sure to curry favor with him. Balladyn will be the one introducing the two of you."

Joy of joys. Bradach would have to act like he was friends with Balladyn. At the rate the day was going, it wouldn't surprise him if Eoghan asked him to become a Dark permanently.

How the fek was he going to complete this mission?

"Can you handle it?"

Bradach was offended that Eoghan would even ask that question. Bradach shot him a flat look. "Of course. But things would go a lot easier if Rhi would do whatever it is that she's going to do to Usaeil. That fight has been brewing for a while between the two of them."

"Not before we find Xaneth."

Bradach grunted at the reminder of the royal. He didn't bother to ask why Xaneth was so important. The simple fact was that Death took care of those she called allies, and the royal was one of those.

So, whether Bradach liked it or not, he would put his neck on the line to find a Light Fae who had aided them on occasion but had really been a pain in their arses.

With a thought, he used glamour to change his black hair and silver eyes to the coloring of a Dark. His jeans and white shirt altered to black pants and a charcoal gray button-down.

"I'll get the information," he promised Eoghan before he teleported to the Fae doorway that led off the realm to Earth.

CHAPTER

two

Tipperary, Ireland

Whoever said it was easy to be a boss had never run a Dark Fae business. Maeve had spent her entire life trying to fill the very large shoes of her father after he'd been murdered. She'd managed it, but in order to do so, she'd had to be ten-times more clever and cruel than anyone else.

It proved to be exhausting.

Yet she'd amassed a business of contraband and trade of all kinds that had doubled the size of her father's. Since the moment she'd taken over, she had been in the spotlight.

First, to see if she would fail. Then, when she succeeded, others tried to topple her. Since that time, more had gone above and beyond to get on her good side. But still, she was watched.

Every move she made, every word she said was dissected by those who wanted to see her fail.

And those who waited to take her business out from under her.

Maeve stood in her bedroom and stared out the large window to the rolling landscape of vivid green grass speckled with white sheep, and the gray rock walls beyond. Once, the position she held had been all she'd reached for. That was so very long ago.

Her business had been solid on the Fae Realm, but on Earth, it soared. Humans helped more than they knew. For a while, they made things interesting, but it wasn't long before she got bored with them, as well.

That was the problem. Nothing interested Maeve anymore. She had done and seen it all. What else was there for her to do?

Have a family?

The mere thought was laughable. The one thing Maeve wasn't, was a mother. Children and babies freaked her out. They were loud and noisy and many smelled. She wrinkled her nose at the thought. She had no idea what to do with kids, so she made sure she kept far, far away.

The doors behind her opened. Her eyes closed, and she let out a soft sigh. She knew what was coming.

"It's time," Leon said.

The annual party she threw had arrived quicker than she would've liked. All she had to do was make an entrance, give a toast, and then she could make a quiet exit. It's what she did every year.

Maeve turned to face her trusted deputy—and only friend. She and Leon had grown up together from the time they were infants. He knew her better than anyone, and she knew him. Which was why she trusted him.

In fact, he was the only person she trusted.

He smiled warmly, showing his affection. His black and silver, shoulder-length hair was pulled back in a queue and tied with a red ribbon. "You look beautiful. But you always do."

She laughed as he had no doubt intended and glanced down at the silver dress she wore that molded to her upper body and hips before the soft, sheer fabric fell gently to the floor. On her neck, ears, wrists, fingers, and even in her hair were glittering diamonds.

"You don't look too bad yourself," she said as she walked to him, noting the black tux with its red lapels. "You know you don't have to escort me."

Leon shrugged. "It's tradition. And you know how I love tradition."

He touched his chest and the amulet beneath his clothes that she'd given him when she took over the business. Leon never took it off. Just one more connection between them, showing their tight bond.

Together, they walked from her office down the stairs to where select individuals had been invited to attend the most coveted party of the Dark Fae.

They stopped outside the large double doors of the ballroom. Maeve stared at them. She loved getting dressed up, but she wished she was doing something she wanted to do instead of mingling with people who conspired against her and planned her death behind her back.

"It'll be over soon," Leon assured her.

She shot him a grateful smile and motioned him away. "I'll see you inside."

Once he was gone, she snapped her fingers. Four Fae appeared carrying a black and silver velvet litter. She waited until they set it down before she climbed onto it, reclining on her side while her elbow held her up.

Then she was lifted, and the doors opened. Inside the ballroom, the music halted, and all eyes turned to her. Her gaze moved over faces, never lingering on anyone for too long. She bowed her head to a few in greeting, but most, she ignored.

When they reached the dais, the litter was lowered, and two Fae held out their hands for her. She took them as the pair helped her to her feet. Once standing, she looked over the crowd.

Her gaze snapped to the right when she caught sight of someone she hadn't expected to see—the King of the Dark.

And he wasn't alone. The man next to him was intensely intoxicating. She wanted to stare at him and take in every detail of him, but she forced herself to look away.

Maeve was curious as to why Balladyn was there—and who his companion was. Not that she could refuse the King.

Oh, she could, but it was a death sentence if she did.

A glass of champagne was held out to her. She took it and softly let the corners of her lips turn up in a slight smile that didn't reach her eyes.

"Thank you all for coming to my party, celebrating another successful year. My father began the tradition, and it is something that I've enjoyed continuing. What better way to spend time with others than an event celebrating the wonderful year we've had?" She lifted the flute high. "Sláinte."

"Sláinte," the audience replied in unison.

Maeve drank deeply, savoring the alcohol. While many Dark saw the humans as nothing more than food, she had come to see them as so much more. In many ways, they enriched her life. The champagne, for one. It was her favorite drink.

There was just something about the bubbly brew that made her happy. Whether it was regular or pink champagne, she loved it all.

Intending to savor the rest of the glass—as well as the bottle—in her bedroom, she turned to walk from the dais. There were too many people. She felt vulnerable, exposed. It was time to leave and return to the safety of her room.

As she approached the steps leading down, her gaze landed on Ardal. He'd been attempting to woo her for six centuries. You'd think he'd get the hint that she wasn't interested.

But he had yet to give up.

Ardal looked impeccable in his tux with his short black and silver hair slicked back. His red gaze locked on her as he gave her a charming smile. There was no doubt he was handsome, and he had a quick mind. He was good at running his export business, as well.

But no matter how much she tried, Maeve wasn't attracted to him. She'd told him that several times already, but he was like a dog with a bone.

"Maeve," he said as he took her hand and helped her down the steps. "You get more beautiful every time I see you."

She forced a smile and looked up at him. "Thank you."

He tucked her hand in the crook of his arm and turned them. To everyone looking, they appeared very much a couple. Maeve planted her feet so he couldn't move her and deliberately pulled her hand away, all while never taking her eyes from his face.

"I thought I made myself clear," she stated.

His smile was tighter than before, proof that she'd hit a nerve. "If you would just give me a chance."

"You don't love me," she said. "You love my power, my position, and my company."

"That's true, but I also have a fondness for you. Shouldn't that be enough?"

She raised her chin and took a deep breath. This was a conversation she'd had many times with those trying to win her hand. "Do you know why I've never married?"

"You've not found the right man," he said with a wink.

She didn't so much as grin. "It's because not a single one of you wants me. You all want what I have. I've built all of this," she said with a wave of her hand. "I took what my father had and transformed it. I didn't need a man then, nor at any time throughout my life. And I don't need one now."

Ardal's face flushed with rage as he became aware of those near them who were now listening intently. Despite Maeve telling him this before, it had always been done in privacy. He was the one who'd pushed her into a corner. And it was time he realized who he was dealing with.

"You're making a mistake," he whispered.

She shook her head. "No, Ardal, you are. You need a woman you can control. I'm not it."

Maeve pivoted and walked away with a glance toward Leon to make sure that Ardal didn't follow her. She only took a few steps before she was stopped again. This time by a young, female Dark.

"I'm sorry," the young woman said. "I know its taboo for me to stop you, and my beau is beside himself that I ignored his warning and came over anyway."

It took balls to do this. Maeve didn't like being stopped. In fact, anyone who dared was severely punished—though it had been years since she'd last done that. The Dark had long memories. It only took a few times for them to understand what she wanted.

But she also remembered being young and trying to find her way. She held up a hand when Leon sent two guards to take the girl away. Then Maeve looked at the female. "And you are?"

"Leena," the girl said with a bright smile.

Maeve looked her up and down, noting the slinky red dress and the stylish updo the woman wore. Then she glanced at Leena's beau, who appeared both shocked and ill as he stared at

Leena's bravery. Maeve didn't recognize him, but that didn't mean anything. She did business with a lot of Fae—even a few Light.

"I hope you're enjoying the party, Leena."

"Very much so," the young Dark replied. Then she leaned in close and said in a low voice, "I've admired you for so long. I want to be just like you."

Maeve used to enjoy when people said that to her. Now, all she could think of was that the person would come after her and her business. One day, it would happen. Someone could only hold the top spot for so long before they were overthrown.

"Do you now?" she asked.

Leena bobbed her head. "I have so many ideas."

"I'm sure you'll be amazing."

"Do you have any advice for me?"

Maeve paused as she recalled what her father had told her—never trust anyone. The guidance had helped her succeed, but it had been a solitary existence only broken by Leon.

Maeve glanced to her right where her faithful friend stood. Except this time, his gaze wasn't on her, it was on a man. They were smiling at each other, the kind of smile that lovers shared. When had Leon taken a new lover? And why hadn't he told her? She felt deeply wounded that he hadn't shared such news with her. Especially when they told each other everything.

Maeve swung her attention back to Leena. "Be careful who you trust. You need people who are reliable and devoted, but in turn, you have to be loyal to them. Treat them good and pay them well. Give them no reason to betray you."

Leena nodded solemnly. "I will do all of it."

Maeve moved past the Fae before Leena could ask anything else. It felt as if the room were closing in on her. She had to get out of the ballroom and quickly. As she approached the door, she noticed that Leon still had eyes only for his lover.

Not once had he ever let her down, and she didn't want it to start now. Leon had always been there for her. Even the times when she hadn't thought she needed him. He had instinctively known what she required. In truth, Leon was indispensable.

No one else stopped her, but that could be because two guards fell into step behind her to make sure that didn't happen. When Maeve reached the side door to exit, Leon wasn't there. It was the first time in . . . too many years to count.

She tried not to be hurt by it, but that's what happened when you counted on someone. Her father had warned her not to do it.

"Depending on others means that you let your guard down. That leaves you weak, because you'll begin to care for them. And that, my darlin' girl, is how they'll betray you and take everything you have."

Maeve walked through the door, her father's words ringing in her ears. She had only taken two steps when Leon suddenly fell in step beside her.

"I didn't see you," he explained.

She halted and looked at him. It took a great deal of effort not to snap at him, but she buried the emotion and kept her tone even. He was her only friend, and she had to remember that. "Your attention was on someone else. I saw him."

Leon sighed and briefly lowered his gaze to the floor. "I should've told you about him. It's new. Very new. It won't happen again."

"I walked through a doorway, not into battle. It's fine." And it was okay. She shouldn't be jealous of her friend finding comfort in someone's arms just because she couldn't. No, she should be happy for Leon.

Yes. She would be happy for him and shove aside any jealousy she had of the time Leon spent with his new lover. None ever lasted long anyway. Though she'd never seen Leon look at someone as he had the man in the ballroom earlier.

"But . . ." Leon said with a frown. "We always leave together."

She smiled sadly. "What is it you're always telling me? The only constant thing in life is change?"

"Maeve," he murmured, his brow furrowing deeper. "I've hurt you. I'm sorry."

She waved her hand between them, cutting off his words. She was upset, but she hated that she felt that way. She wouldn't give in to the emotion or let her friend know of it. "Return to the party as you always do and have a nice night."

But Leon didn't move. He rubbed a hand over his chin. "Ardal will retaliate for what you did to him."

"You mean what he did to himself?" She shrugged, uncaring. "Let him. And we'll see who comes out the victor."

Leon chuckled. "He's not the first, and I daresay he won't be the last to try and win you."

"Don't you know, old friend? I don't have a heart for anyone to steal."

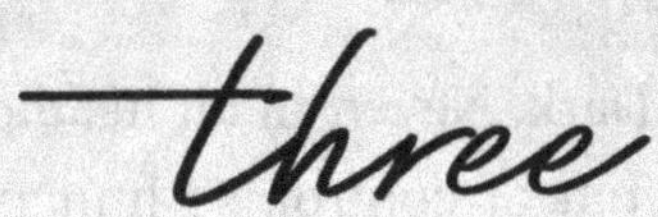

F ek.

It was the only word on repeat in Bradach's head from the moment Maeve arrived in the ballroom. The moment his eyes landed on her, he hadn't been able to look anywhere else. She was so stunning that she took his breath away. Literally.

She had a face so flawless that he couldn't look away. Kohl-lined, almond-shaped eyes lifted in the outer corners to give her a seductive look. High cheekbones and full lips outfitted in blood red made his cock twitch.

And hunger rush through his veins so hot it scalded him.

Then she stood from the litter. Her voluptuous curves molded by silver fabric made his balls tighten. It was a primitive response, unadulterated and utterly primal.

She moved forward, and his eyes lowered to the impossibly high slit that went up her right leg. He heard a chuckle beside him, but he didn't pay attention. No, Bradach was listening to her sexy voice that made his heart race.

There was no denying the attraction he felt.

And he hated her for it.

He hated Dark—all Dark. Never, in all his thousands of years, had he ever felt so . . . out of control, so hungry . . . for a Dark female. The possibility that he might be attracted to one had never entered his mind. But now that he was faced with it, he had to get himself together.

Somehow.

His eyes focused on her cleavage thanks to the dip in the front of her gown. His hands itched to grab the fabric and yank the dress apart so he could see all of her. He forgot where he was, why he was there, and that there were others in the room—right up until he felt the elbow in his ribs.

"Lift your damn glass," came the whispered demand in a voice laced with irritation.

Bradach blinked, his control back in place as he pulled his gaze from Maeve. He cut a glance to Balladyn to see if the King of the Dark had noticed. The two hadn't said very much to each other once Bradach had gotten to the Dark Palace, but if Balladyn had seen him ogling Maeve, he kept it to himself, only giving Bradach a stern frown. Bradach swallowed, inwardly shaking himself, and noticed the rest of the room toasting Maeve. Bradach hurried and lifted his glass, completely at a loss as to what had come over him.

Balladyn drank down his champagne in one gulp.

Bradach twisted his lips, stopping just short of rolling his eyes. "Oh, that was nice. Very kingly."

The King of the Dark raised a brow as he turned to Bradach. "You've made it abundantly clear that you don't care for me, and I hate to break it to you, gobshite, but I'm not fond of you either. I gave my word to Erith that I'd do this, so I will. That doesn't mean I have to be pleasant."

Bradach looked down at the glass in his hand when he heard the crystal crack. He forced his fingers to relax one at a time. Then he lifted his gaze to Balladyn. "It's not you personally."

"Well, that makes me feel so much better," the king stated acerbically while rolling his eyes.

"It should."

Red eyes cut his way. "It doesn't. So, suck it up, buttercup. We're both stuck."

When Balladyn walked away, Bradach quickly followed despite wanting to go the other way. "What are you doing?"

"She never stays," the king threw over his shoulder.

Bradach glanced toward Maeve to see a man talking to her. By the look on her face, she was none too pleased. And within moments, it became clear to the entire room that she was putting the Dark in his place.

Balladyn backtracked and stood beside Bradach. "She's a ballbuster, but Ardal deserves it. Trust me."

Bradach glanced at Balladyn. "I don't exactly have a choice."

"Remember that," Balladyn stated icily.

Bradach fisted his hands. He was always the cool-headed one. But there was something about Balladyn that made him want to put his fist through the king's face.

With no other choice, Bradach followed Balladyn out of the ballroom when all he wanted to do was continue watching Maeve. While some might throw their power and might around, she wore it like a crown—majestically and regally.

She said nothing, just gave someone a look that would stop them in their tracks. The Dark Fae guards shifted as if expecting her every move, which he assumed they did. That meant they had been with her long enough to know what to anticipate without her having to issue a word or even cast a look in their direction.

But the real trick was watching how everyone in the room stared at her. Most lusted after Maeve—both men and women. There were a few whose jealousy shone brightly in their eyes, and he'd bet his favorite dagger that Maeve was aware of each one.

A woman like Maeve didn't get into such a position without knowing little details like that. It was the envious types that made a bid for whatever they wanted. A few might try to win her over, like Ardal, but most would simply attempt to dispose of her any way they could.

The problem was, Maeve was too dominant. She was influential and held sway with others just as formidable as she. The only way Maeve would be removed from her position was if she gave it up herself. That's how powerful she was.

Bradach and Balladyn moved as silently as ghosts as they walked down the rug-lined corridor. The castle was beautiful. Bradach hated to admit it, but the various shades of silver and black rugs and furniture went well with the gray stone. He particularly liked the carpet lining the hallways. It had just enough metallic sheen to it so that you didn't mistake it for something other than what it was—silver.

"You walk this place as if it's yours," Bradach said.

Balladyn chuckled softly. "I'm King of the Dark. That affords me many things."

"I'm not sure Maeve would agree."

"She saw us."

Bradach's gut clenched at the reminder. Maeve's red gaze had skimmed over him during the toast, but she had lingered on Balladyn for a heartbeat. Why did that anger him so?

He didn't care about Maeve.

No, it was all lust—the hot, all-consuming kind—that he felt.

For fek's sake, he really had to get his body under control. He was disgusted that he was attracted to a Dark. A Dark! He swallowed the bitterness that filled his mouth as he recalled a couple of moments from the past to remind himself why he hated the Dark so.

And just like that, the lust ebbed away into nothing. He was grateful because he never wanted to think about it again. And he would never tell a soul about it.

"How do you even know where she's going?" Bradach asked.

Balladyn quirked an eyebrow as he glanced at him. "Where else but her chamber?"

Bradach couldn't stop his eye roll.

They said nothing as they continued down the long corridor, but Bradach wasn't fooled. The King of the Dark might look as if he were at ease, but he was anything but.

When they approached a set of double doors, Bradach's steps slowed. "You don't actually plan to go inside."

"I do." Balladyn halted before the doors and turned to look at Bradach. "I can't tell you how many times the Dragon Kings, as well as the Reapers, have shown up in my chambers unannounced."

With that, the king used his magic to open the doors. Bradach didn't feel right going inside. Not because it was rude, but because it was Maeve's chambers, and he had just gotten his desire in check. He wasn't ready to test it just yet. Instead, he stood against one of the doors and folded his arms across his chest to wait. He glanced inside to find that Balladyn had taken one of the chairs in the middle of the room.

Bradach could see very little of the chamber from his position. He didn't know how large it was, but he suspected it was grand in size. The manor itself was impressive, and no doubt Maeve would have taken the grandest chamber for herself.

The color scheme of the castle continued into Maeve's rooms, except there was a new color added—white. He wanted to look around at his leisure to learn more about her, which just irked him. He shouldn't want to know more about her. He was there for a mission, and the mission only. Bradach squared his shoulders and remained at his spot by the door.

He knew the moment Maeve turned the corner and saw him. Bradach's head snapped in her direction to find Maeve standing two hundred feet from him, her red gaze locked on him. For several heartbeats, their gazes held.

Then, slowly, her eyes moved through the open doors.

Bradach's lowered his gaze to get another look at the shapely, bare leg that peeked through the slit in her gown when she began moving his way. Her black and silver hair swayed with her every move. He liked the way it undulated sensuously against her arms and back.

The closer she got, the more he was able to see the black ring around her deep red irises. He'd never seen a Dark's eyes that color before. They were . . . beautiful and unusual—just like she was. He'd seen a lot of gorgeous women, but he'd never encountered one who wore sexy like a second skin.

He wasn't even upset when his lust came roaring back. His arms slowly lowered to his sides as she drew closer. He noted the silver stilettos she wore. He quite liked the way the shoes made her legs look. And the fact that she walked with such confidence in five-inch heels somehow made him desire her even more.

She held his gaze as she came even with him. Maeve paused to stare at him. Bradach saw an eyelash on her cheek and reached up. She pulled her head away, her eyes narrowing slightly. But he didn't lower his arm. He raised a brow, silently daring her to knock his hand away.

Was it his imagination, or did her lips curve slightly? By the stars, this woman was going to drive him mad, he craved her so. She held still as he retrieved the long eyelash and held it out for her to see. To his surprise, she grasped his wrist and blew the eyelash from his finger, just as he'd seen countless humans do.

The feel of her hand on him was like a jolt of something hot and electric running straight to his cock. He bit back a groan just in time.

Before he could react, Maeve released him and proceeded into her chamber. Bradach turned with her, utterly mesmerized.

By a Dark.

He could hardly believe it. Later, when he got himself in check again, he would be sickened by it all. But for now . . . all he could do was try not to give in to the raging desire.

But the knowing smirk on Balladyn's face told Bradach that the king had seen every fekking minute of what had transpired.

"Wonderful," Bradach murmured beneath his breath.

Maeve entered her chamber, walking like the queen of her own domain, and then elegantly sank into one of the white, stuffed chairs opposite Balladyn. "What brings the King of the Dark to my home?"

"I thought you'd demand to know why I'm in your chamber," Balladyn said with a grin.

She crossed one lean leg over the other and took a drink of champagne from the glass in her hand. "I was getting to that. I thought it prudent to ask what you want of me first."

"And if I said I wanted you in my bed?"

Bradach jerked his gaze to Balladyn, fury ripping through him so fiercely that Bradach had taken a step toward Balladyn before he realized it. He stopped himself, but the king was ignoring him. It was the sound of Maeve's laughter that drew Bradach's eyes back to her.

"I needed that laugh," she said. "Thank you. You have all the women you could want, my king."

Balladyn smiled charmingly and rested one arm on the back of the chair. "And I wouldn't want you?"

Yep. Bradach hated Balladyn. Loathed him.

"No," she said with a shake of her head.

Bradach was shocked to see a flash of sadness in her eyes. He hadn't expected that.

"I'm not the only one who has their choice of partners if what I saw in the ballroom is any indication," Balladyn said.

Maeve lifted her shoulders. "Ardal has been after me for a long time. He doesn't understand the word no. However, I'm not usually someone who airs things like that in front of others."

"He left you no choice."

She blew out a breath, resignation filling her face. "That he didn't."

Bradach's lungs seized when her eyes slid to him for a heartbeat, then two. He wished he knew what she was thinking. He wanted to call her attention back to him, but he wasn't sure why. He hated Dark Fae. All Dark.

Didn't he?

The more he stared at Maeve, the more unsure he became.

What was it about this one female that could alter his thoughts so drastically?

Bradach leaned his head to the side as he regarded her. He was so wrapped up in trying to figure out what made her different that he nearly missed Balladyn speaking.

"I wanted to introduce you to my friend, Bradach."

"Oh?" she asked but didn't look his way.

Bradach tried not to be offended. Attempted and failed.

Balladyn's lips twisted briefly. "Bradach is . . . different from other Dark."

"How so?"

It was on the tip of Bradach's tongue to remind them both that he stood right there. Yet, somehow, he managed to keep his lips locked and awaited whatever Balladyn would say. It was as close to trusting a Dark as Bradach would get.

He almost snorted aloud.

"I think you should find out for yourself," Balladyn replied.

She uncrossed her legs and leaned forward so that her elbows rested on her knees. "I'm sure you can understand when I say that I don't trust anyone."

"Those of us in such positions can't." Balladyn's gaze moved to Bradach then. "And yet I trust him."

Bradach was so shocked that a feather could've knocked him over. He thought it might've been said in jest, but by the way the king stared at him, Balladyn had spoken the truth. That made Bradach look at Balladyn differently.

"You tell me that why?" Maeve queried.

Balladyn shrugged one shoulder and turned his attention back to her. "I've known of you for a long time, Maeve. I had to keep an eye on you because Taraeth was wary of a woman having as much power—both in magic and position—as you."

"And when you became king?" she pushed.

One side of Balladyn's lips lifted in a grin. "You've given me no reason for concern."

"Good. I have no interest in your throne."

His lips widened into a smile. "You already have a throne. In many ways, you have more worries than I."

"Yes," she said, her eyes dropping to the floor for a moment.

Balladyn got to his feet and turned to Bradach. The king held his gaze as he walked to him and told Maeve, "I know I came uninvited. I apologize for that, but it was the perfect place and time for us to meet." He turned and looked at Maeve when he came to stand beside Bradach. "I must return to the palace now. However, I request a small favor."

"You want me to talk to Bradach?"

Even now, she wouldn't look at him. Bradach was moving from being offended to downright angry. Why wouldn't she meet his gaze when she hadn't had a problem before? Was there something on his face?

"Yes," Balladyn said.

She rose to her feet in one fluid motion. "I will grant this favor for one in return at a later date."

"I expected no less." The king inclined his head and teleported out.

Leaving Bradach alone with a woman he didn't know whether to kiss or walk away from forever.

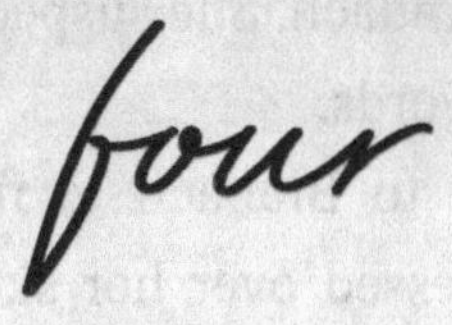

With no one else to look at, Maeve had no choice but to turn her attention to Bradach. Her cheek still tingled from his light touch earlier.

He made her edgy and nervous, agitated and unsettled. She knew each time his gaze was on her. Wherever it touched her, warmth spread over her like a caress. She only wanted to look at him, to learn every detail of his features—which was why she had made herself not look at him.

She couldn't remember the last time anyone had made her feel such things. She wanted more of it, but at the same time, it frightened her because she had no control over it.

Desire.

Yes, that's what it was. Raw, unadulterated yearning. A craving so deep and so profound that Maeve couldn't ignore it. Her body reacted on a primeval level, one that was instinctive and intuitive.

Bradach hadn't said a word since she arrived, but she'd seen the perturbed look he'd given the king.

The fact that Balladyn had also seen it and not reacted said a lot about both men. Some might think it made Balladyn weak, but she saw something different. Perhaps it was the way the king had told her that he trusted Bradach. She suspected there was a lot that wasn't said in those few words.

She turned her head to Bradach to find him watching her. Once more, his gaze caressed over her skin and left chills in its wake. She wanted to move closer to him, but she didn't dare. She didn't trust herself to keep her hands to herself.

No matter how hard she looked, she couldn't tell what he was thinking, and that bothered her. She had a way of seeing past the masks that others put up. Not so with Bradach.

His short, black hair laced with silver was longer on the top and sides, showing her the wavy texture. His red eyes were direct, probing—and gave nothing away. But his face . . . she held back a sigh.

He had a square chin with a dimple in it and a strong jawline that she loved. His face was clean-shaven, showing his wide mouth and thin lips that she wanted to see turned up in a smile.

Already her pulse was racing, and she hadn't even gotten to linger her gaze over his tall form.

"An endorsement from the king is high praise indeed," she said.

Bradach bowed his head toward her. "As long as you think so."

Her knees went weak at the sound of his voice. It was deep and smooth and sexy as hell. Maeve swallowed and lowered herself back into the chair before her legs betrayed her. That way, she could concentrate on keeping control since it was becoming an issue with every second she was around Bradach.

"Why does Balladyn want me to talk to you?" she asked, then motioned to the chair for him to sit.

He stared at the seat Balladyn had used earlier before he walked to it with measured steps and slowly sat.

"Can I get you something?" She lifted her champagne flute that was now empty. "Something to drink, perhaps?"

"Thank you, but I'm good," he replied.

She raised a brow, waiting for him to answer her first question. While she did, she let herself look over his body. He was tall and had an easy confidence that she rarely saw in others. His tuxedo jacket showed off the width of his shoulders, and she wondered if it hid as fine a body as his face.

"I'm searching for someone," he finally said. "It's important that I find him. He's a friend, and I fear he's in trouble."

She hadn't expected this. Maeve frowned as she set the flute on the glass table next to her. "I'm a little confused, and I think perhaps Balladyn is, as well. I'm not in the business of finding people. The king has more pull than I do."

"It's not what you can do for me. It's who you know. Your connections."

It was the careful way that Bradach worded it that had warning bells going off in Maeve's head. "You think I know someone who can help you?"

Bradach leaned forward in his seat and trapped her gaze with his. "I wasn't clear before. Let me try again. I'm hoping that you know the person who took my friend."

"I see," she said, nodding slightly.

"He needs to be found. And quickly."

"Why?"

Bradach blinked, taken aback by the question. "Why?"

She laughed softly. "Yes, why? You said he's a friend, but why must he be found?"

"Because the person who took him intends to kill him."

"I see." That put things into perspective. "When was he taken?"

"A few weeks ago."

Her eyes widened. "And you think he might still be alive?"

"The one who took him hasn't been seen either, which is not the norm."

It was something about the way he said the words that made her frown. "Who is it that you believe took him?"

He drew in a breath and then slowly released it. "Usaeil."

It all made sense now. She held Bradach's red gaze. He was hiding something, a big secret. One that he would die for. She could see it there in his eyes, in the way he held himself, waiting for her to say something. How had she missed it before?

Because she'd been drooling over his face and body, that's how.

"I see," she said.

He narrowed his eyes on her as he cocked his head to the side. "If you don't know her, tell me now. I'll not waste any more of your time. But . . . if you do know her, I can make it worth your while to help me."

"Let's say I do know her. What could you possibly give me that I don't already have?"

"Quite a lot, actually."

Now that intrigued her, and few things did these days. Dammit. "Like?" she pushed.

He glanced at the floor. "Let's just say that I know someone very powerful and that this deed will not go unnoticed."

"You mean the king?"

"Balladyn, yes, but also another."

"There is no one more powerful than the King of the Dark."

Bradach said nothing, which made Maeve all the more curious. He seemed certain that he knew of someone, and that fascinated her. She not only wanted to know who it was, but it would also be stupid to pass up an opportunity to gain something for herself.

Then again, there was Usaeil.

"Continuing our hypothetical conversation, I would be signing my own death warrant if you can't win against the Queen of the Light."

"Do you think she's stronger than Balladyn?" Bradach asked.

Maeve clasped her hands together in her lap. She didn't know Bradach, and while the king might trust him, the truth was, she didn't know Balladyn either. She shouldn't be talking to either of them about anything as volatile as Usaeil.

Because Maeve knew firsthand what the Queen of the Light was capable of.

Bradach gave a shake of his head at her silence. "You wouldn't be wrong."

"I didn't say anything."

"You didn't have to. The answer was the one you refused to utter." He turned his head to look out the door and down the hallway. "I'm not here as some spy for the queen or Balladyn. I'm here because I need to find my friend. He's been gone for too long already."

Maeve didn't have to wonder about the lengths she would go to if someone kidnapped Leon. She would do anything and everything in her power to find him. But years of reading people for a living told her that there was much Bradach wasn't telling her.

None of it may involve Usaeil or Balladyn. Or all of it might. She didn't want to get mixed up in something like that. It was messy, and people were often betrayed left and right. She had worked too hard to build what she had.

And yet . . . there was a part of her that wanted to help Bradach. Whether it was the way he kept looking at her, his sensual voice, or his words, something tugged at a place inside that she hadn't felt in eons.

"You're sure it's Usaeil who took him?"

Bradach nodded solemnly. "He's her nephew."

"I didn't see that coming," Maeve said and blew out a breath. "I thought all her family was gone. At least, that's the rumor I heard."

"She made sure her family was . . . gone," he said with a knowing look. "Xaneth is the last."

"That's a feat in itself. How did he survive?"

"He's smart," Bradach said with a snort. "He lived by moving between the Light and the Dark. You might have heard of him. He's known as the Seeker."

Maeve chuckled softly, nodding. "I do know of him. Matter of fact, he's worked for me before. He always came through and kept his word. His name is Xaneth? I never asked, and he didn't volunteer it. Royalty, huh?" She thought back to the last time she had interacted with the Seeker. The way he'd held himself, the way he spoke. "I can see that now."

"He not only evaded death at Usaeil's hands, but he also betrayed her."

That wiped the smile from Maeve's face. "I don't like those who betray others."

"Sometimes, it's a necessity. He deceived her in order to save the life of a Halfling that Usaeil was out to kill."

"With all these deaths, how is it that Usaeil is still Light?"

Bradach's brow quirked. "That is a question, isn't it?"

"One you know the answer to but won't give me."

"You know the answer, as well."

Maeve blew out a breath. Damn, she wasn't sure she wanted to know all this information. "She's Dark and hiding it."

"Aye."

Maeve looked toward the ceiling. "None of this makes sense. Why would Usaeil pretend to be Light? Well, that answer is simple. Power. She likes ruling over others. That's obvious by the way she rid herself of anyone in her family who could take the throne."

Maeve's gaze lowered to Bradach. "She rules the Light. But someone that power-hungry who would go to such lengths to hide their real identity wants much more."

Bradach gave a little tilt of his head for confirmation.

"Does Balladyn know this?" she asked, suddenly worried for her new king. She liked Balladyn, and she never thought she'd ever say that about a King of the Dark.

Bradach snorted. "Balladyn knows a lot more than anyone gives him credit for. He has his own agenda against Usaeil. He and Xaneth are also friendly, so he wants Xaneth found, too."

Maeve raised her brows as she began putting pieces of the puzzle together. "Balladyn was a general in the Light army and is now sitting on the Dark throne. With what you've told me about Usaeil, assuming I believe you, it wouldn't be too much of a stretch to think that the queen had something to do with Balladyn becoming Dark."

"Balladyn's story isn't for me to tell. I can see why you would be hesitant, but I will do whatever you ask in order to gain your trust."

"But you know Balladyn's story."

"I do."

They stared at each other for a long moment, then she asked, "The simple fact that Usaeil is a Dark masquerading as a Light says a lot about her. Again, assuming you're telling the truth."

"There are those who have seen her eyes flash red when she gets angry. Yet, as much as I need your help, I should warn you that getting tangled in this could mean the end of your life if Usaeil discovers what you're about."

Maeve hadn't had such a challenging job in a long time. She wanted to shake up her life some and get out of the rut she currently found herself in. A lot of her desire had to do with the sexy Fae sitting across from her that she couldn't stop looking at.

Or imagine kissing.

"I can handle myself," she said.

Bradach grinned. "Assuming I'm telling the truth."

She couldn't help but return his smile. "Precisely."

The longer she was with Bradach, the more comfortable she was. As if she had known him for hundreds of years instead of for just a few minutes. She'd never had that kind of connection with anyone. Usually, she was much more guarded.

"You look worried," he said. "Wondering how I'm going to prove all of this to you?"

"Now that you mention it, yes."

"That will require you to use glamour while we visit the Light."

She jerked back. "Have you lost your mind? We'll never get away with that."

"Yes, we will. Unless you aren't up for the challenge," Bradach said, his red eyes sparkling with the dare. "I thought the great Maeve would never back down from anything. Especially nothing so . . . calm . . . as using glamour to walk among the Light."

She regarded him for a full minute in silence. Somehow, he knew exactly what to say to get her to do what he wanted. Leon didn't even have that ability, so what made Bradach different? There was a fair amount of danger in joining Bradach in this. Usaeil could see it as Maeve taking sides. But Maeve was so bored, maybe this was just what she needed.

"As if I could let something like that go," she said. "All right.

I'll join you. And you better hope for your sake that what you say is true. Otherwise, favor to the king or not, I'll exact my revenge on you."

"Sounds intriguing," Bradach said with a crooked grin that made her heart beat double-time.

She'd wanted her life shaken up, and she was getting exactly that with Bradach.

Gods help her. Because she liked every second of it.

CHAPTER
five

The idea had come upon him unexpectedly. Bradach didn't regret his plan to bring Maeve to the Light. If he could walk among the Dark, she could do the same with the Light.

Not only would he have a good chance of convincing her that he was telling the truth, but she might also see another side to the Fae that she didn't know.

Bradach didn't want to think why that seemed important. He knew it was rare for a Dark to turn Light, but it did happen. Is that what he wanted? Would he then feel better about being attracted to her?

Fek, but it was all so damn confusing.

"I suppose you want to go now?" she asked.

She shifted her legs, causing him to look down at the slender limbs. He imagined running his hand from her ankles up to her thighs and shoving the dress aside to see her. His cock hardened.

"Aye," he said and then cleared his throat as the picture of his thoughts took root.

Maeve gave him an odd look before raising a brow. "Is everything all right?"

"It's perfect."

She got to her feet and looked down at her gown. "I believe I need to change."

"A shame. You wear the dress well."

A pleased look filled her features. "I'll return shortly. Make yourself at home."

Bradach watched as she turned and walked away. His eyes followed her through a doorway that he suspected was her bedroom. He then got to his feet and looked around the chamber. It appeared they were in a living area of sorts.

Besides the doorway Maeve had disappeared through, there was another on the opposite side behind him. He wondered what was through there. It would take but a second to discover the answer, but he didn't check.

It was a good thing because, in the next moment, Maeve returned. She was in a pair of white pants that molded to her shapely legs. He noticed the white heels, but it was the black and white horizontally striped tee with gold lettering that said Lady Boss that made him smile.

She shrugged on a short black jacket with three-quarter-length sleeves as she asked, "Do you approve?"

"I do. Don't forget," Bradach said and motioned to his eyes and hair.

A brief frown flashed across her face. "Right. I'd forgotten."

She snapped her fingers, and the silver vanished from her hair. He'd thought he would like it better, but somehow, the silver added something that made it distinctly hers. Then there were her eyes. The black-ringed deep red was gone, replaced by silver.

Though there was nothing plain about her orbs. They were bright, as if she were lit from within.

"You look almost disappointed," she replied with a chuckle.

He quickly shook his head, masking the distress he felt at his thoughts. "Not at all."

She crossed her arms over her chest, making him take note of the gold bangles on her wrist. "And you?"

As if he could forget. He let his glamour fall away to reveal his true self, all the while never taking his eyes from Maeve's face. She didn't so much as twitch.

He wasn't sure what he expected, but he'd thought she might do . . . something. Or maybe he was just so wrapped up in his lustful thoughts that he wasn't thinking clearly. That had to be it.

Bradach's tux fell away to be replaced by a green button-down, dark denim jeans, and his favorite boots.

Maeve walked closer to him, her gaze running up and down his body. "Hmm. I'm wondering if there's something you can wear and not look good in."

His body was on fire with need as her gaze raked over him. No one had ever complimented him in quite that fashion before. He liked it. A lot.

"Thank you."

"You appear comfortable as a Light," she pointed out when she stopped before him. "You've done this many times before, haven't you?"

Bradach shrugged in answer. He didn't want to lie to her. It shouldn't be an issue, but it was. And he didn't know why. He'd never had a problem lying to a Dark before. Why did it have to crop up now?

Maeve reached behind her, gathering her long hair high on the back of her head before securing it. "You intrigue me. I'm beginning to suspect you're like Xaneth and move between the Light and Dark with ease."

"I wouldn't say that."

"Mmm," she replied. Then she inhaled quickly. "Where are you taking me?"

"There are a couple of places actually, but we'll start with Dublin."

Her brows came together. "Dublin? There are plenty of Dark and Light there. Why that city?"

"I plan to show you." He held out his hand, waiting for her to take it.

She hesitated a moment before she met his gaze and placed her palm in his. As soon as she did, Bradach teleported them to Dublin.

He didn't remember why the Fae had chosen Ireland as theirs, but he couldn't imagine another place on the realm where the Fae could be happy. And just like in their home world, they split the land. The top portion was Light, and the bottom Dark.

Dublin was near the invisible border that had been drawn eons ago by the Fae. And while that divide kept most of the Light and Dark in their respective areas, there were those who ventured to the other side. Dublin was a city that had plenty of Light and Dark Fae wandering the streets, mixing in with the humans.

As soon as they arrived, Maeve pulled her hand from his. Bradach instantly missed her touch. He looked around the city. There was something about it that he liked. It kept him coming back again and again.

"Come," he told her when he spotted what he was looking for.

Maeve fell into step beside him. "You know I've been here before, right? Why do I need to look like a Light?"

"How much do you pay attention to the human world?"

She shrugged as she glanced his way. "Some."

"Do you watch their movies?"

"Of course," she said with a bark of laughter.

He stopped before the newsstand and faced her. "Then you know."

"Know what?" she asked, confusion lining her face.

"About Usaeil."

Maeve blinked. "I don't know what you're getting at."

Bradach pointed to one of the magazines. Maeve followed his hand to read the headline. Her eyes widened, and she took a step back in shock. He quickly put his hand against her back to steady her and prevent her from running into a man.

"That's a picture of Usaeil," Maeve whispered while staring at the magazine cover.

Bradach moved them closer and looked around to make sure no one could overhear them. "You said you watched movies. I naturally assumed you knew."

"I've watched some. It's not something I do all the time." She turned her head to him. "How didn't I know that Usaeil had immersed herself with the humans?"

"It's easy to miss," he said with a twist of his lips.

Maeve read one cover after the other, each one with a different picture of Usaeil, all asking where she had disappeared to. Maeve picked up one of the magazines and flipped to the story inside to read it. Bradach stood beside her while scanning the area for any Fae.

He spotted two Dark and numerous Light, but no one seemed to have noticed them yet, which he was grateful for.

Maeve was well known. He didn't want anyone seeing her masquerading as a Light or be asked questions neither of them could answer.

"I have no words," Maeve said as she put away the magazine and faced him. "Do the Light know?"

Bradach shook his head. "A few in her Queen's Guard know, but no one else."

"How did you find out?" Maeve pressed. "Are you as immersed with the humans as she is?"

He jerked back, offended that she would even say such a thing. "No."

"Then how did you learn of this?"

Bradach looked away, clenching his teeth. How did he tell her without lying? What could he say that would be the truth? Then he found it. "I've a source who gives me such information."

"You trust this source?"

"Absolutely."

She flattened her lips briefly. "Now that I've learned this, what's next?"

He held out his hand again. She took it instantly, and he teleported them outside the Light Castle.

"You can't be serious," Maeve stated.

Bradach grinned. "Very much so."

They began walking toward the entrance. Not a single Light Fae looked twice at them. If Maeve was nervous, she hid it well. Then again, a woman in her position would've learned to mask such things long ago.

"How did you meet the Seeker? Xaneth, I mean," Maeve asked.

"A mutual acquaintance. He ended up helping us."

She quirked a brow. "Us?"

"My friends and I."

"Right," she said with a nod of her head. "To save someone Usaeil wanted to kill."

Bradach smiled at her as they passed through the large double doors into the castle. Maeve's gaze moved from side to side, taking it all in. She smiled and nodded to others who looked her away. If Bradach didn't know any better, he'd believe she was a Light.

"Care to tell me who this person was that you saved?" she asked.

Bradach waited until there weren't so many around before he leaned in close and said, "I don't think I can."

"You're not sure you can trust me, you mean."

There was no heat in Maeve's words, which surprised him. He nodded. "There is a lot at stake and I—"

She stopped and faced him as she held up a hand. "There's no need to explain. I understand. You're trusting me enough to tell me the things I need to know in order to help you."

"And you're trusting me to take you where we need to go."

"Don't think I'm not prepared if you try anything to harm me," she warned.

Bradach frowned, affronted. "I wouldn't do that."

"You wouldn't be the first to try."

She had no idea that he was a Reaper, or that his magic and power far exceeded hers. To her credit, she believed he was just a normal Fae, which meant she knew she could best him.

He cocked his head to the side. "If you feared I might do something to harm you or take you somewhere to trap you, why did you come with me?"

"Normally, I wouldn't. But . . ." She sighed loudly. "I haven't quite figured out why I agreed. I'm no fool, though. As I said, I've dealt with enough assassination attempts to know how to handle myself."

The thought of her continually looking over her shoulder unsettled him. It made her joining him even more special. "I think you're far from a fool. You've amassed an empire. No one does that by being reckless."

"That's right," she said with a confident smile.

If he hadn't already had the hots for her, he would now. Damn, but he loved a self-assured woman. "Since you're still alive, that means you've thwarted all your would-be attackers."

Her gaze darted to the right. "I'm still standing, yes."

It was her lack of an answer that alerted him. "How close have you come to dying?"

"As if I'd tell you that," she said with a laugh and began to walk away.

He couldn't decide if he was furious with or worried about her. Bradach grabbed her upper arm in a light hold to stop her. He moved closer and brought his face within inches of hers. "You should never have agreed to come with me."

"Why? Because you plan to hurt me?" she demanded, her eyes glittering dangerously.

"Never. But you don't know me. I could have."

She lifted her chin. "I follow my instincts about people. Balladyn's endorsement would have meant nothing if my gut had told me you were something other than what you presented."

That's when Bradach realized that despite not wanting to lie to her, he'd been doing so from the very beginning. And that bothered him greatly. His gaze dropped, and he found himself staring at her plump lips.

In that instant, he comprehended just how close their bodies were.

And how easy it would be to lower his head to take her lips.

CHAPTER

six

He was going to kiss her.

Maeve held her breath, waiting for Bradach to close the short distance between them. She forgot about being in the Light Castle, forgot about the discoveries being made about Usaeil.

Everything faded until it was nothing but Bradach and her.

As she gazed into his silver eyes, she saw the band of white around his irises. It looked like a starburst. She had the insane urge to run her finger along his chin and delve into the dimple there. Being near him made her forget all the rules she had made for herself.

Indeed, the gut-wrenching attraction made her reckless.

The sound of someone approaching caused Bradach to glance in the direction. The spell around them was abruptly broken. She stepped back, pulling her arm from his hand, distancing herself physically and mentally from him.

"Maeve," he whispered.

She looked at him, waiting . . . hoping . . . She didn't know for what exactly, and that made everything worse.

"Why are we here?" she asked after clearing her throat and inwardly giving herself a shake.

Bradach stared at her without answering.

She waited until the Fae they'd heard walked past, then she looked expectantly at Bradach. "You brought me here for a reason. What is it?"

"I wanted to show you the Light."

"Why?" she demanded.

He looked away. "It's another way for you to get to know Usaeil."

"I know her."

"You think you know her," he stated, his gaze jerking back to her.

Maeve crossed her arms over her chest. "She's a queen. She was never going to let me know the real her. Parts, maybe. But not all."

"Just like you don't let anyone know all of you?" Bradach retorted.

"No one wants to know me."

"Some might."

Maeve held up a hand to stop their insane conversation. She wasn't even sure how they had gotten into it. "This isn't about me. I've had dealings with Usaeil. And, yes, I asked questions earlier because I like to know what I'm getting into. But the simple fact is, I'm Dark. I couldn't care less about the Light. My king introduced you and me and asked me for a favor."

"You don't care about any Light?" Bradach asked softly, something sparking in his eyes.

"You heard me correctly. My loyalty lies with the Dark."

He blew out a breath, a flash of disappointment in his silver eyes. "Then we're wasting time. Tell me what you know about Usaeil."

Maeve fought not to roll her eyes as she pivoted and retraced her steps out of the castle. She didn't even try to teleport out. Most likely, the building had wards to prevent that.

Once she reached the place where Bradach had brought them initially, she spun to look at him. No anger showed on his face, but she felt it nonetheless. She didn't know what she had said that had roused his ire, and she didn't care.

She didn't.

It didn't matter. Once she finished giving him the information he needed, she wouldn't see him again. She'd make sure of it.

Because Bradach made her think of things she had given up on long ago.

Dangerous things like companionship and . . . love.

"I won't do this here," Maeve told him, suddenly uncomfortable with all the Light moving about. She took hold of him and teleported them.

When they reached the destination she had in mind, she watched Bradach look around at the tall junipers that swayed in the wind before he turned and glimpsed the hillside covered in grapevines.

He swung his gaze to her. "Where are we?"

"Napa Valley, California. A place Usaeil mentioned to me once as being a destination she retreated to when she wanted to disappear."

"Did she say where exactly?"

Maeve shook her head. "She's a queen, used to having the best of everything. She won't be in anything less than the grandest place."

Bradach lifted his eyes and gazed past her to look around him. Maeve could leave now. He didn't need her anymore. She had given him the information he wanted. In fact, she could've given it to him at her home. But she hadn't.

Because she'd wanted to get out of her rut.

She'd certainly done that. And in the process, she'd discovered that she lusted after him. She'd had plenty of sex in her life, but there had never been a relationship. Never anyone who made her crave their touch or hunger for their nearness.

Nor had she ever fallen asleep with anyone before. She'd made sure her partners were out of her bed before that could happen. There was a line with falling asleep in your lover's arms that she never wanted to cross. She did it to protect herself and her business.

Why then did she keep wondering how it would feel to be wrapped securely in Bradach's arms as she drifted off to sleep?

His head shifted so that his gaze once more snagged hers. She had no idea what he was thinking, and she hated that. Perhaps it was for the best, though. Remaining with him put everything she'd worked so hard for in jeopardy.

"Good luck with your hunt," she told him.

His brows furrowed in surprise. "You're leaving?"

"You have what you need."

"No," he said with a shake of his head. "You gave me a location where she could be, but that doesn't mean she will be here. I'd rather you stay while I check things out. You might remember something else or another place."

Her heart leapt at the idea, though she reminded herself it was out of necessity, not because Bradach wanted her beside him. If Usaeil wasn't in Napa, then Bradach would have to return to talk to her to find another hideaway the queen might have.

"All right," Maeve replied as pithily as she could.

They made their way to the empty house that sat for sale on the ridge overlooking a portion of the magnificent valley. They both paused, basking in the beauty.

"How often did you and Usaeil spend time together?"

Maeve had wondered when this question would come. She was surprised it hadn't been voiced sooner. "My main business is with the Dark, obviously, but there are times I have dealings with the Light and humans. That's how I met Usaeil. She came to me for a business deal. I knew who she was, obviously."

"You'd seen her before?"

"I make it my mission to know the top players among whoever I'm dealing with, especially the Fae. Usaeil didn't tell me who she was at first. It took her a while before she admitted it. Since I knew she was expecting me to act as if I were excited about having her as a client, I pretended as if the name meant nothing."

Bradach looked shocked as he turned his head to her. "She believed you?"

"Most anyone in positions of power like to have their ego stroked."

"You're in a position of power."

Maeve laughed. "Perhaps, but I'm referring to a king or queen. Usaeil likes to be recognized. She likes to have others fawn over her. It makes sense now that she would go into the human world as an actress. The mortals would give her all the attention and devotion she requires."

"That is definitely Usaeil."

"And completely opposite of Balladyn."

Bradach raised a brow. "Really? You know him that well?"

"Not as well as you. First, he was a lieutenant to Taraeth, and then king. He has his own way of ruling, something that is vastly different than anything the Dark have seen before. But it's working. He's fair, and while he can be harsh at times, he has to be. Just as he has to have a foreboding look about him. Otherwise, he'd never last."

"You like him."

She nodded, not denying it. "You sound surprised. But, yes, I do. I also respect him. He's done wonders for the Dark in a short amount of time. But you know all of that as his friend."

"Right," Bradach said off-handedly.

Maeve studied him as he looked away. "You don't sound so sure."

"I am," he said hastily and shot her a smile.

She swallowed, not totally convinced. "What are you going to do when you find Usaeil and Xaneth? The queen's incredibly powerful."

"You saying I can't take her?" Bradach asked with a teasing grin.

Maeve didn't return it. "I'm saying she'll cut you down instantly."

His eyebrows shot up on his forehead. "Concerned for my welfare?"

Maeve wanted to deny it, but she couldn't. There was just something about Bradach that she had instantly taken a liking to. "Maybe. I don't like wasting my time helping you, only to see you die."

"She won't know you aided me. I'll make sure of that."

Maeve was outraged that he'd believe that's what was on her mind. "I didn't mean that at all."

"It's something anyone would think about. No need to be angry about my assumption. As you said, Usaeil is powerful."

Maeve rolled her eyes, wishing they could drop the subject. "Everything dies eventually."

There was a long pause, then Bradach said in a deep voice full of wrath, "She'll never touch you."

Maeve's gaze swung to him to see the promise on his face. "You're just a Fae, Bradach. You can't stop her. You might be able to free your friend, but she'll come for you. You have to know that."

"I hope to hell she does."

"You want to die?" Maeve asked in shock.

Bradach shook his head and looked forward. "I won't be the one dying."

"Who are you to make such claims?" she demanded.

"No one."

"Liar."

He blew out a breath and dropped his chin to his chest. "Maeve, I can't tell you. Please, don't ask."

She swallowed, her mind trying to figure out who he could be, but nothing she came up with seemed to fit or make sense. "I suppose we should start looking for Usaeil."

"As soon as we find her location, I want you to return home," Bradach ordered.

Maeve immediately took exception. "It's been an extremely long time since anyone's told me what to do. You're not going to start now."

"I can, and I will. Because I won't have the queen taking your life simply because you showed me where she might be hiding. Promise me you'll leave," he urged.

It was on the tip of her tongue to continue arguing, but she knew it would be pointless. "I'll leave."

"Good," he said with a relieved smile.

"When we have Xaneth."

Bradach's face hardened with anger. "Did you not just hear anything I said?"

"I heard it clearly, actually."

"Then why do you want to dance with certain death? Because that's what you'll be doing."

She shrugged, laughing. "I have no idea. Maybe I've been sitting on the sidelines directing others for too long. Maybe because I want to help bring down someone like Usaeil. Or maybe because I just want to help you."

"I knew it was a mistake to ask for your help the moment I first saw you," Bradach said softly. "You're obstinate and tenacious. Even if I get you to leave, you'll return, won't you?"

She gave him a big smile. "I'm impressed. Most wouldn't have figured that out about me."

"Maeve, you're going to regret knowing me."

"I'm pretty sure I already do." It was a lie, but he didn't need to know that.

Bradach ran a hand through his hair and blew out a loud breath. "Stay near me at all times. I have to have your word on this."

"And if I don't give it?"

"I'll send you back to your mansion right now. Fek," he murmured. "It's what I should do anyway."

He was the first person she honestly believed could send her back and keep her there. But that's not what she clued in to. "Then why aren't you doing it?" she pushed.

Bradach held her gaze for a long minute before he finally said, "It doesn't matter why. I have a mission."

"Then why are we still talking about it? Let's find Usaeil."

CHAPTER

seven

It was a mistake. A huge blunder that was going to come back and bite him in the arse. Hard. Bradach knew it as surely as he knew that the woman beside him had him by the balls.

The only saving grace was that she didn't know it.

Yet.

He tried not to look at Maeve, attempted not to think about how good it felt when he held her hand. And if that felt so good, he knew it would be amazing when she was in his arms.

"Fek," he said under his breath.

He was so screwed. What had he been thinking, wanting her with him? Oh, he could tell himself that it was to save time, that he didn't want her warning Usaeil, or any number of other lies.

But that was exactly what they were—lies.

The simple—and gut-wrenching—truth was that he liked having Maeve with him.

Liked! What the fek was wrong with him? She was a bloody

Dark Fae, and he couldn't get enough of her. And gods help him, he hadn't even kissed her yet.

He inwardly cringed. Yet. How fekking laughable. If he had his way, he'd be tasting her lips right now instead of searching for the grandest house in the area. He'd have Maeve naked and beneath him while he kissed and caressed her entire body. His cock twitched as he imagined sliding into her.

"You think you'd be happier that we're closing in on the queen," Maeve said as she glanced in his direction.

Bradach swallowed and tried to think of anything but her naked. He couldn't. He didn't need Maeve asking questions, especially since he seemed to have a problem with telling her a lie.

"I am happy," he ground out.

She snorted. "Sure."

Each time they teleported, she touched him, which was a special kind of hell. Bradach had stopped reaching for her since it was too painful to feel her soft skin beneath his palm and know that was all he should do—all the while craving so much more.

They were at the fifth estate when something made him pause. He took a second look at the house. "This is it."

"It's gaudy enough," Maeve said in distaste. "But I'm not convinced."

He didn't reply as he studied the area. It was only a few moments later that he saw a veiled Light—or what used to be a Light Fae. No matter how powerful a Fae was, the only ones who could remain veiled for longer than a few minutes were Reapers. And the Light was far from one of them.

Ordinary Fae could only stay veiled for about thirty seconds. Those like Balladyn and Usaeil could be veiled for closer to three minutes. But, eventually, the magic failed them.

There were other perks to being a Reaper besides the added

power and magic given by Death. Bradach was able to see anyone who was veiled—and their true face.

The Fae Bradach watched now was changed, his skin ashen. Bradach had a suspicion it was one of the creatures that Usaeil created. Xaneth had told the Reapers about how the queen had used the Trackers to hunt and kill her family. Xaneth himself had watched as a Tracker killed his little sister. The royal's brief description of them was what led Bradach to believe that's what he looked at now.

"What do you know of Usaeil's Trackers?" he asked Maeve, never taking his eyes off the creature.

She shook her head. "They're nothing but rumor and speculation. Some lie someone told to scare others."

"I hate to tell you that they're real." He pointed to the Fae that was about to lose his veil.

The moment it dropped, and Maeve saw him, her brows drew together in a deep frown. "That's not a Light or a Dark. What is that?"

"Tracker. Also sometimes called Usaeil's Hunters. I think we need a closer look."

She gaped at him. "Who's being reckless now? You know nothing about this being, and yet you want to go down there and attack it."

Bradach grinned and lifted one shoulder in a shrug. "Actually, I thought I'd get his attention while you took a closer look at the house for any sign of Usaeil."

It was a perfect plan. He could fight as he needed to without Maeve watching so she wouldn't guess how powerful he was. And he'd learn more about the Trackers. Then again, he should've known that she wouldn't readily agree.

"You want to call that thing up here?" Maeve asked with a

quirked brow, her face lined with skepticism. "That will undoubt-edly alert other Trackers, Usaeil, or both. And," she said, drawing out the word. "You want me to go have a look."

Bradach glanced at the mansion. There was a very good chance the queen was there, and if she was, she might come out to investi-gate the disturbance. He wanted to see her so he could know for sure if Xaneth was there.

His eyes swung back to Maeve. However, he wasn't willing to risk the Dark. He hadn't seen Maeve fight, and while he suspected she could hold her own since she'd survived many assassination attempts, he wasn't willing to test that theory without being beside her to help out if she needed it.

And there he was, willing to help a Dark again.

What the hell was going on with him?

"No," he said.

Maeve pressed her lips together as frustration filled her face. "What? I thought you wanted me to look at the estate?"

"I do. Did." Fek. He needed to get his shite together. "I've changed my mind."

Her eyes narrowed. "Don't try and tell me to leave."

"It'd be best if you did."

"I'll admit, you look as if you could take on a couple of Trackers. But more?" She shook her head of black hair. "I'm sorry, but not even Balladyn could do that."

Bradach thought back to the king when he joined them in their battle with Bran. And he actually grinned. "You'd be surprised."

Then he winced when he realized that he'd said the words aloud. First, the attraction to Maeve, and now admiration for Balladyn? It was like the world had been turned upside down, and Bradach wasn't sure how to handle that.

"Obviously, there is much about my king I don't know," Maeve said with her arms crossed over her chest and her head tilted to the side.

"You won't leave, will you?"

She shook her head, her gaze daring him to try and make her.

Bradach blew out a breath. "I want to see if Usaeil is here. Because if she is, Xaneth will be, as well."

"He'll be surrounded by her magic," Maeve pointed out.

"Making it difficult to get to him. I'd really like to find him first before I alert Usaeil to the fact that anyone is here."

Maeve grinned. "Which means no killing the Tracker."

"Which means, no killing the Tracker," Bradach repeated testily.

He debated on whether to alert Eoghan to what he'd found. Usaeil and Xaneth could be in the mansion, but it could also be a trap—for the Reapers and anyone who helped him.

Bradach eyed Maeve. "Did Usaeil freely give you the information about this place?"

"Freely?" she asked, wrinkling her nose. "I don't think I'd put it that way. Usaeil liked to talk about all the places she went, boasting about the things she did and the lovers she left in her wake. I never prodded her for anything because I didn't think she'd tell me. It was during our seventh meeting, which ran for several hours, that she mentioned she had a couple of hideaways. Places that no one knew about."

"If no one knew of them, why tell you?" Bradach asked.

Maeve shrugged. "At the time, I thought it was because she liked me. Now, I'm not so sure."

Bradach returned his attention to the mansion. It was the details that always stuck out for him, just as Eoghan had mentioned. And while Bradach couldn't pinpoint what it was, something was missing.

"You think it's a trap," Maeve said.

He shrugged without looking at her. "It could be."

"We won't know unless we have a look."

Bradach reached over and stopped Maeve when she took a step forward. Then he turned his head to her. "If anyone is going down there, it's me."

"I can handle myself."

"I'll go because it's my mission."

Her jaw set. "Need I remind you that you brought me into this?"

"I'm extremely aware of that."

Instead of getting angry as he expected, her face smoothed out. "I can take care of myself, I assure you."

"I'm sure you can."

"But?" she asked when he hesitated. She searched his face when he didn't reply. "You believe you can handle it all by yourself."

He didn't answer. Nothing he could say to deny or confirm it would make things better.

"Who are you?" she asked, her brow puckered.

Bradach dropped his arm. "Someone trying to save a friend."

"Xaneth must be really important for you to risk so much. He's a royal everyone has believed dead all these centuries. Why does his life matter?"

"Every life matters."

She stared at him silently. "Spoken like a Light."

Fek. Fek fek fek.

Bradach drew in a deep breath and changed the subject. "Did Usaeil mention the location of her other hideaways?"

Maeve shook her head.

"Thank you for your help, but you should return to your home."

"And find out you died because no one was here to watch your back?" she asked.

Bradach smiled wryly, though her words touched him. "Worried about me, huh?"

"Maybe."

He had the urge to reach up and stroke her cheek. "Don't be. I won't be alone."

She shoved away a lock of hair that had fallen into her eyes. "First, you can't talk me into joining you fast enough, and now you can't wait to be rid of me. It's enough to give someone whiplash. Go do whatever it is you do. Good luck, Bradach. Whoever you are."

Maeve teleported away before he could say his farewell. He wanted to call her back, to tell her . . . Hell, he didn't know what he wanted to say, but he didn't like that she had left so quickly. Maybe it was better that way since he wasn't sure if he could keep from kissing her.

Yes, it was definitely better with her gone. Now he could focus on the task at hand. If only the image of her face would stop popping into his head.

If only he could stop thinking about how bright her eyes were.

If only he could stop thinking about how he actually liked the silver in her hair.

If only he could stop thinking about how nice it had been to have her beside him.

If only he could stop thinking about what might have been. . . .

He drew in a deep breath before he released it and faced the mansion. Then he veiled himself. Bradach didn't know everything

Bran might have told Usaeil about the Reapers, but regardless, she didn't have the power needed to stop him.

Or keep him out.

Bradach stalked toward the structure. He walked past the Tracker, noting the pallid skin and milky white eyes against the stark black hair. Just what were these creatures? And what could they do?

No sooner had the thought gone through his mind than the Tracker halted and lifted his face as he sniffed. As if . . . smelling for Bradach.

Bradach stilled. He could easily kill the Tracker and take it to the other Reapers so they could see what this was. But a missing Tracker, whether Usaeil was in Napa or not, would alert her that someone had been there.

No matter how much he wanted to end the creature, Bradach made sure to keep two feet between them. To help mask the sound, he moved when the Tracker moved, which was good, because not only did the being seem to have enhanced smell, he also clearly had heightened hearing.

The creature pulled back its lips to show sharp fangs. Usaeil had obviously been up to something, and it was time these beings were eradicated.

Bradach heard something behind him, but he didn't turn to see what it was. He didn't have long to wait as the noise drew closer. It was the sound of sniffing that alerted Bradach it was another Tracker.

"Someone's here," the one in front of him said.

There was a grunt of agreement from behind him.

He felt, rather than saw the Tracker behind him. Bradach bent backwards as he saw the hand come at his face from the one in front of him. It passed within an inch of his head but never connected to him. A moment later, Bradach straightened while shifting to keep both creatures in his sights.

"It's this place," the second one said. "Nothing smells right."

"There's someone here," the first insisted.

The second gave a shake of his head and walked away. Bradach remained with the first even when it continued on its rounds of the grounds. That allowed Bradach to get a glimpse inside the house.

The Trackers didn't speak much. In fact, they said very little to each other, almost as if they preferred to be alone rather than in groups.

Bradach counted four of the beings. He learned a great deal about their cat-like movements, which were quicker than any normal Fae. With their heightened hearing and sense of smell, few would be able to escape them. This was all information the Reapers would need to know when the time came to battle them.

Because that time would come. Bradach was sure of it.

Now, all he needed to see was how their magic stacked up.

CHAPTER

eight

"I knew it," Maeve whispered to herself as she hid behind a tree on a hillside overlooking Usaeil's property.

She'd never had any intention of returning home. Bradach had been too sure of himself. There were only two kinds of people that had that kind of confidence: The ones who had never been in a battle.

And the ones who had been in many—and knew just how good they were.

Bradach was the latter. She'd bet her entire fortune on it. Which was why she'd remained behind. He hadn't wanted her to know something, and she knew that he wouldn't do whatever he needed to if she was around. The solution had been to pretend to leave.

She just couldn't believe he'd bought it.

Her suspicions about Bradach were realized when she saw him vanish. At first, she believed he'd teleported, but when she spotted the Tracker acting weirdly, she decided to watch it. That's when she saw it sniffing the air and tilting its head as if listening for something.

Like someone walking near it.

It didn't take a great leap to believe that Bradach was veiled. The only problem with that was that no Fae could hold it for longer than thirty seconds, with the exception of the king and queen, who could manage about three minutes each. Yet, Bradach had surpassed that and then some. Though she couldn't figure out how.

If Balladyn and Usaeil couldn't do it. . . . Well, Maeve wasn't certain Usaeil couldn't. Or Balladyn, for that matter. But if either of them could, news of it would've spread like wildfire through the Fae. Since it hadn't, then Maeve would continue to assume that neither of them could.

So, how in the world was Bradach doing it? If he was powerful enough to do that, then he might have the strength and magic to defeat Usaeil.

But . . . why? Typically, anyone who had that kind of power used it for their own purposes. Bradach didn't seem to have any interest in Balladyn's throne. And while she could imagine Bradach being hired to take out Usaeil, the king didn't seem the type to let anyone do his dirty work.

Which left what, exactly?

Maeve searched her mind for anything that Bradach had said in the short time they'd been together, anything that seemed odd. She snorted. Everything he'd said seemed unusual. He, himself, wasn't like any Fae she'd ever met.

He might be Dark, but he acted like a Light on some occasions. Hell, he looked damn good as a Light, as well.

Her thoughts traveled to his fine body—without clothes. Her

mouth watered just thinking about running her hands over every hard inch of him.

She shook her head to clear it and to get her thoughts back on track. Bradach had mentioned others when he spoke. Family? Friends? Both? She wasn't sure, but while he might be here alone, she didn't imagine he was usually like this. In fact, she got the impression that he was part of some sort of group.

Her thoughts ceased when she spotted the second Tracker. The two stood facing each other, both creatures intent on the air between them. The spot she sincerely hoped Bradach wasn't standing.

She gasped when one Tracker swung a hand toward the space. Maeve just knew the being was going to connect with Bradach, but somehow, the Tracker had missed him.

Or Bradach was just that good.

Maeve smiled because she had a feeling that the Fae was, indeed, that good.

Her heart started beating normally again when the second Tracker walked away. The first seemed determine to suss out Bradach, but after a little while, he gave up and went back to patrolling.

Maeve had no idea where Bradach had gone. She kept her gaze on the Tracker until he moved out of sight. For all she knew, Bradach could've left already. But that didn't mesh with the Fae who had been determined to locate Usaeil—and thereby, Xaneth—at all costs.

He'd even used the King of the Dark to aid him. There was no way Bradach would give up so easily. No, he was down there at the mansion, probably getting a close look at the structure to see if Usaeil was there.

Maeve wished there was a reason for her to go down to the

house and knock on the door, but there were so many variables and so many things that could go wrong. She could use glamour to change her appearance, but she didn't want to test that in case Usaeil was the one who opened the door.

Undeterred, Maeve made her way through rows of grapevines to move to a better position to see the side and back of the mansion.

She'd just gotten situated in a new spot when one of the Trackers whirled around and stood straighter as a back door to the house opened. From behind the grapevine and with the large shrub blocking the side of the house, Maeve couldn't see who spoke to the creature.

She did make out a bright yellow shirt through the foliage, though. Then, as luck would have it, the person moved forward. The moment they came out from behind the shrub, Maeve knew it was Usaeil.

If only Maeve knew where Bradach was to tell him. But there was one way to let him know.

"Bradach."

To say a Fae's name was like making a phone call. They heard it and were able to go to the person who had summoned them, but it was up to the Fae to do that.

The fact that Bradach hadn't appeared meant that he didn't wish to talk to her. That greatly disappointed her. She had expected better of him.

"What the hell are you doing here?"

She froze at the sound of the voice behind her. Then, a second later, she recognized it as Bradach's. Maeve slowly straightened and turned to find him with his arms crossed over his chest and a scowl on his face.

"I'm admiring the view," she stated.

"I thought you were returning home?"

Maeve couldn't remember the last time she had been afraid of anyone, and she certainly wasn't now. At the scowl on Bradach's face, most people would be. She raised her chin defiantly. "You thought wrong."

His arms dropped to his sides as he shook his head, his brow furrowing. "What were you planning to do?"

"Make sure to watch your back since I knew you'd do something . . . reckless."

His gaze searched her face. "What did you see?"

She knew what he was asking. It was on the tip of her tongue to lie and say nothing, but she chose another route—the truth. "You can veil yourself for long periods of time."

"Fek," he muttered and ran a hand through his hair as he turned away to pace a few steps before whirling back to her. "You should've left as you said."

"I did leave."

His face went hard with anger. "You know what I mean."

"Yes. I do," she said by way of apology. "I'm good at keeping secrets, Bradach. I won't tell anyone what I saw."

But he didn't seem to be listening to her. His eyes had moved to the mansion. "That's Usaeil."

"That's why I called you," she explained.

He came up beside Maeve and pushed them down into a squat a heartbeat before Usaeil's gaze swung their way. Maeve couldn't figure out how he'd known what the queen was going to do, but she was glad that Bradach had. Otherwise, Usaeil might have seen them.

As it was, the queen's gaze lingered on the slope as if she knew they were there while trying to pinpoint their location.

"If she's here, does that mean Xaneth is, as well?" Maeve asked.

A muscle jumped in Bradach's jaw. "Most likely. I won't know until I get into the house."

"That should be easy for you."

His lips twisted ruefully. "I've had a bit of a run-in with Usaeil already. She'll be expecting me."

"Does she have wards up around the house?"

Bradach's silver eyes swung to her. "Actually, no. I felt nothing."

"Then it's a trap. She'll wait for you to get inside before she tries to keep you there with magic."

He gave a loud snort. "That won't work."

"Then maybe it isn't you she's after."

Bradach's face went slack. "Fek me. You're right."

Maeve wanted to ask just who it was that Usaeil wanted, but she managed to hold back. Besides, Bradach likely wouldn't tell her. She thought she kept secrets, but he held many, many more.

His gaze met hers. She smiled because she knew what was coming. "You're about to tell me that it's time I really do return home. And that if I don't do it, you'll bring me there yourself."

"It's not because I don't want you here," he hurried to say.

She shrugged. "You think I'll either get in the way or get hurt."

"No," Bradach said with a shake of his head. "There are things you can't know, things you can't see."

"Like your veiling ability."

He remained silent, which was answer enough.

"I see," she said, disappointment filling her.

She had looked forward to fighting beside him, but that was something she would never get to do. She'd imagined that in her head all the while Bradach intended to make sure that she never would.

Maeve had always lived her life on her terms. She wasn't about to change that now. She flashed Bradach a bright smile. "Good luck. I expect a visit from you and Xaneth when this is over."

"You assume I'll win," Bradach replied with a grin.

She held his gaze, hating to leave. Not only did she enjoy his company but he also intrigued her. Something that hadn't happened in a very long time. She gave him a wink and then teleported away.

Except she didn't go home. She arrived outside the Dark Palace. Maeve looked at the huge structure. It had been a while since she'd last been there, which perhaps hadn't been a good move on her part.

She made her way inside, stopping at the entrance. Her gaze moved around the area, noting the guards and the other Dark milling about. The palace wasn't just different from the Light Castle in color, the people were distinct, as well.

While she hadn't realized it when she was in the castle, Maeve recognized that the atmosphere was much lighter. There was still deceit, as there was in all courts, but it wasn't the same heavy, foreboding kind that filled the palace.

Maeve didn't want to go to the throne room and wait to be seen along with many others. She wanted to talk to the king now. But there was only so much daring she'd do, and going to Balladyn's chambers as he'd done with her was pushing it.

"Balladyn," she said softly.

Then she waited. It was only a minute later that a guard made his way to her and told her to follow him. She was taken up several flights of stairs to the top of the palace and then down a corridor to a set of doors taller than any she'd ever seen. The guards at the doors opened them and stepped aside for her to enter.

She walked inside and quickly glanced around to see if anyone else was there. When she found the chamber empty, she walked to the tall windows and looked out over the land. The view was absolutely stunning.

"I knew you'd come. I just didn't expect it to be so soon."

Maeve really was getting tired of people coming up behind her, though this time, she blamed herself. She should've known the king would do just that.

She turned and curtsied.

Balladyn chuckled at her obeisance. "Care for a drink?"

"Please," she said and let her gaze move around the spacious room. She noted the library at one side and the multitude of books lining the shelves. She glanced in the other direction but didn't see a bedchamber.

Balladyn walked to her and held out a tumbler filled with a shot of whisky. "Why don't you tell me what brings you here."

"I want to know about Bradach."

CHAPTER

nine

They were here. Just as she'd known they would be.

Usaeil grinned as she stared at the slope of the hill. The Reapers would be in for quite a surprise when they tried to free Xaneth.

She'd wanted to kill her nephew as she had the rest of her family, but she'd changed her mind at the last second. Usaeil realized that Xaneth could be used for something else—bringing the Reapers to her.

Bran had failed. She'd thought for sure the ex-Reaper would be able to take out Death. She didn't know whether it was Bran's overconfidence or his lack of planning that had caused it all to fall through his fingers. Not that it mattered. Bran may have been powerful, but he wasn't royalty.

He couldn't compare to the magic that ran through her veins. She'd proven her might century after century, war after war.

And had he bowed down to her as she demanded, she might have stayed with him to fight. Yet he'd shown his true colors. He didn't want a partner. He'd wanted to rule her—something that would never happen.

Usaeil had made sure of that many lifetimes ago. She wasn't going to let some brainless egomaniac with women issues take that from her. Besides, the moment she saw Xaneth, she forgot everything else but the need to kill him.

"My queen?"

She swung her head to the Tracker nearest her. "You said you smelled someone."

"Aye," he said with a bow of his head.

"How many?"

His black brows drew together. "Just one."

"For how long?"

"Twenty minutes or so, but I found no one."

She grinned and stepped closer to the Tracker. "The person will come again. Don't alert the intruder that you know they're here. The moment you smell them, let me know. Tell the others to do the same. I want the trespasser to think he's fooled everyone. Do you understand?"

"Yes, my queen."

Usaeil turned on her heel and reentered the house. The place was grand, but it was nothing like the home she'd grown up in on the Fae Realm. In fact, there wasn't much about Earth that could compare to everything she'd lost on her home world.

The recreation of the Light Castle was nearly an exact replica of the ruins in the Fae Realm, but not even that could dull the never-ending ache of missing her world.

No matter how much the Fae took over this realm, it wasn't theirs. That much had been painfully clear from the moment they'd found it. Back then, she'd been in favor of ridding Earth of the Dragon Kings.

But all that had changed. She could see the bigger picture now. This world was a good match for the Fae. And combining the Dragon Kings with the Fae would make a dominant race of beings that no one could ever defeat.

It was the Kings who kept the Fae from destroying Earth as they had their own realm. Usaeil wished she could take credit for that, but after the Fae Wars, few of her race—even the Dark—wanted to go up against a Dragon King.

They were formidable enemies.

But the Kings would do anything and everything for allies. So, she'd made sure the Light sided with them. Together, they had effortlessly defeated the Dark. And for a while, the peace was what she'd thought she wanted.

It wasn't long before she craved . . . something, though. She wasn't sure what it was. All the eons of battle with the Dark had kept her focused on that. She'd dreamed of a time when the two sides could live almost harmoniously.

The Kings had given her that. And yet, it wasn't enough. She grew bored with everything. The mind-numbing duties of being queen, the constant requests from her people, and a life so boring, she would return to what was left of the Fae Realm just to scream her frustration.

The only solace was Rhi. The Fae's light shone brighter than anything Usaeil had ever seen before. And to her astonishment, Rhi had caught the attention of a Dragon King. The attraction between the two had been so strong that anyone near them had been ensnared in its storm.

Somehow, despite being rather ordinary, Rhi had found something . . . extraordinary. Usaeil failed to curb her jealousy. Then she'd begun to notice how others treated Rhi, how they looked at

Rhi with awe and worship—exactly how they were supposed to look at her!

Usaeil halted her thoughts as she closed her eyes and clenched her fists. She couldn't let herself go down that road. Not now. She would become lost in the fury of it all. It wasn't time for that. But soon.

Very soon.

She drew in a calming breath and released it as she loosened her fingers. Then she opened her eyes. She smiled at how she had gotten herself back under control.

After another moment, she continued walking. Her feet took her up the stairs and down the corridor to a room in the far-left corner. She opened the door and entered before softly closing it behind her and making her way to the bed.

She stood beside Xaneth, who lay on his back, still as death. It was fitting that her torture of him was taking place in his mind. No matter what he did, he would never outrun her. It was a torment that could—and would—last for eons.

And in many ways, it was better than death.

He'd managed to evade her Trackers. Xaneth had then made a nice life for himself with the Light and the Dark. But the real kicker was when she had hired him to kidnap Thea. She hadn't recognized who he was then, but once she had, she'd been confident that he would never betray her.

But Death and the Reapers had convinced him to do just that.

Usaeil had never intended to let him live. He had a purpose, and once he served it, she planned to end his life. There would be no one of her blood left alive to take the throne from her.

Not that it mattered if there was. She was powerful enough to get rid of anyone who even dared think about ruling the Light. With the plans she had for the Fae and the Dragon Kings, it was better if all the little . . . secrets . . . of her past remained just that—secrets.

She sat in the chair near the bed and crossed one leg over the other. For so long, she'd been as terrified of the Reapers as every other Fae. And for what?

Absolutely nothing.

Death had been in her castle along with the Reapers, and not a single one of them had been able to take her. They hadn't even followed when she ran, which told Usaeil all she needed to know about the so-called strength of the Reapers.

Everything about them was built on hearsay. There was no one around who could attest to what they could really do. And if Death were as commanding as she was supposed to be, she would've stopped Usaeil.

Usaeil laughed at the thought of the petite woman in her black dress trying to stop her. It would never happen. And if Death and the Reapers knew that, then it was time everyone else did, as well.

Usaeil reached over and touched Xaneth's shoulder. He jerked, his back arching. That was the only sign he exhibited of the torment he suffered in his mind.

Xaneth would be an example of what happened to people who betrayed Usaeil. With Xaneth locked in such agony, he could never speak of who he was, which meant that she would keep him forever. She'd bring him out as a threat to keep others in line.

In fact, such an imprisonment might just be what was in store for Rhi.

"No," Usaeil stated emphatically to herself. "The bitch has to die."

So much of the discord between Usaeil and the King of Dragon Kings was because of Rhi. Usaeil had had Constantine in her bed. He'd been her lover.

And what a lover Con was.

Usaeil smiled as she thought of the ecstasy he'd brought her. And the pleasure she'd brought him. Because no matter what Con said, she knew that he'd been well satisfied. There wasn't anything anyone could say that would dissuade her from believing that.

Then Rhi just had to go and ruin it all.

The wrath that flooded Usaeil had the force of a tsunami. It roiled through her, burning brighter every second, every hour of every day. The longer Rhi went without being punished, the darker Usaeil's anger became.

Rhi, who had pretended to be Usaeil's friend. Rhi, who had made her believe that she didn't have a care in the world other than being the first female member of the Queen's Guard. It had all been a lie.

It was Rhi who wanted Usaeil's throne. It was Rhi who coveted the respect and admiration that was Usaeil's right. It was Rhi who had dared to love a Dragon King.

Rhi. Rhi. Rhi! RHI!

Usaeil grasped her head with both hands and squeezed her eyes shut. Everywhere she turned, everywhere she looked, she saw that interfering, self-righteous twat.

Rhi had fooled everyone, but she wasn't the darling all thought her to be. There was darkness in her. Usaeil had sensed it the last time they spoke. No doubt it had been there all along, and Rhi hid it. But she wouldn't be able to do that for much longer.

Everything was Rhi's fault. Usaeil wouldn't have had to betray Balladyn to Taraeth if he hadn't let it slip that he loved Rhi. Usaeil wouldn't have had to kill Rhi's brother if he hadn't discovered how she made Trackers.

And she wouldn't have had to tear apart Rhi's relationship

with her King if Rhi hadn't fallen in love before Usaeil had secured her own Dragon King.

Usaeil dropped her hands and opened her eyes. She was going to take great pleasure in killing Rhi. But before she did, Rhi was going to lose everything.

All the friends she believed Usaeil didn't know about. Rhi would watch them die slow, painful deaths.

Usaeil knew Rhi would call out to her lover. No matter what the Light said about hating him, Usaeil knew the truth. A love like that could never die. She was counting on Rhi to bring him to the battle.

While Usaeil couldn't kill a King, he could—and would—watch Rhi die. And there would be nothing he could do about it.

That's how all Fae and the Dragon Kings would realize Usaeil's might. She would then merge the Light and Dark into one race once more. And after that, she and Con would be mated.

Together, they would rule this realm supreme.

Her aspirations didn't stop there, however.

Usaeil looked at Xaneth. He looked too comfortable. She stood and leaned over him so that her mouth was next to his ear. "You can run, nephew, but I'll always find you."

The tree limbs clawed at his face and body as Xaneth rushed through the forest. He had no idea where he was. It had been days —or was it weeks?—since he'd last seen the sun.

No matter how many times he attempted to teleport, he always ended up in exactly the same spot, again and again. That's how he knew that magic held him. And it didn't take him long to guess who was responsible—Usaeil.

But he wasn't alone in this horrid place. Something was chasing him. It had caught him once. He glanced down at his abdomen. The four slashes that ran diagonally across his chest and stomach had yet to heal properly. No doubt they wouldn't as long as Usaeil's magic held him.

He gave a final push through the dense brush and found another tree to lean back against. His lungs burned, and his midsection stung from the cuts. But he couldn't stop to see to the wounds or give his body a rest.

It had been so long since he'd slept. His eyes closed on their own, and a second later, he was drifting off to sleep. It was the sound of Usaeil's voice in his ear telling him that he could run but never hide that jerked him awake.

He spun around, his head moving from side to side, looking for her. She wasn't there. He knew it, but for that moment in time, it had felt as if she stood right beside him.

The roar of the beast was close. Too close. Xaneth turned and started running again.

CHAPTER
ten

A booming silence followed Maeve's statement to Balladyn about Bradach.

The king stared at her for a long time before he walked to a chair and sat, motioning to the other. She had no choice but to take it. For another minute or so, neither said a word as they sipped their whisky.

Finally, Balladyn said, "You don't want to know about Bradach."

"I do," she insisted.

He shook his head. "No, Maeve. You don't."

"You make it sound as if I might be offended by what he's done. I'm Dark, my king. There isn't anything you could tell me that would shock me."

Balladyn snorted slightly, his brows raised. "I beg to differ."

"You know, though. Don't you?"

"Aye," he said as he sighed.

She finished off her whisky with one swallow and set the glass on the side table next to her. "He's . . . different than anyone I've met before."

"In what way?"

"In every way," she replied.

Balladyn swirled what was left of his whisky in his glass. "I knew you'd help him. I take you being here to mean that he found the queen?"

"Yes. But he wouldn't let me help him get Xaneth free. Maybe you should go to him."

"Bradach doesn't need either of us."

That caught her interest. "Against Usaeil? You can't be serious."

"I am," Balladyn stated and looked down into his glass before draining the alcohol.

Maeve waited for his gaze to meet hers once more before she asked, "Who is he?"

"Someone you want as an ally. And someone you're better off knowing very little about."

"You almost make it sound as if I should be afraid of him. I'm anything but."

Balladyn held the tumbler in one hand as he leaned forward to rest his forearms on his knees. "That's the mistake you both made. He needed your help, so he had to befriend you. In the process, he intrigued you, so you want to know more."

"And you're telling me that I can't."

"That's exactly what I'm telling you."

She couldn't understand why everyone was being so secretive. But she wasn't without resources. If the king wouldn't give her information on Bradach, then she'd look into him herself. It's what she should've done in the first place, instead of coming to Balladyn.

"Thank you for your time," she said as she got to her feet.

Balladyn was in front of her in a split second. His red eyes blazed as he narrowed them on her. "Don't do anything stupid, Maeve. It's not your style."

"You make it sound like my life could be in danger. From Bradach? I don't believe that."

"Believe it," the king replied.

She gave a nod and then teleported back to her home. Maeve was taking off her jacket when she heard her name. She turned to find Leon sitting in one of the chairs in her chamber.

"Where did you go?" he asked softly.

She smiled at him and shrugged. "The king asked for a favor, and I couldn't refuse."

"But you didn't tell me," Leon said as he pushed to his feet.

The concern in his gaze made her regret causing him to worry. "I told you to go enjoy your night. You don't need to be by my side all the time."

"That's how it's always been."

"And that hasn't been fair to you," she said. "You'll always be my lieutenant, but you should also have time for a life of your own."

He shook his head. "That's not what I want."

"The look you gave your new lover said otherwise."

Leon rubbed the back of his neck and gave her an apologetic look. "Maeve, I've dedicated my life to you."

"And look what we've achieved. I couldn't have done half of this without you. I've thanked you, but words don't seem to be enough. You deserve some time off."

He took a step back, his face shadowed with anxiety. "You want to be rid of me?"

Maeve sighed loudly, feeling weary to her very bones. "The

opposite, actually. I want you to remain my deputy, but if you don't have some downtime, you'll begin to resent me."

"I never have before."

"Then let's not start now. I swear, Leon, no one could replace you. No one," she asserted.

He nodded slowly. "What favor did Balladyn want?"

"He had a friend who needed my help."

"Hmm. You can't exactly say no to the king. Now I know why he was here. I didn't recognize the man with him, though. I suppose the Fae realized in order for you to help him, he needed to enlist Balladyn's help."

She nodded and kicked off her shoes before picking them up and taking them to her bedroom. "Exactly."

"What did you do?"

Maeve didn't know why she was suddenly on edge. It wasn't a question Leon hadn't asked before. While she didn't tell him everything, there was very little that she kept secret from him. He was privy to nearly everything regarding her business. That's how much she trusted him.

Why then did she feel as if he were prying into her life? Into Bradach?

"They were looking for someone," she answered.

Leon followed her into her bedroom and leaned a shoulder against the doorframe. "Someone the king couldn't find? That's odd."

She shrugged and hung up the jacket after replacing her shoes on the shelf. Maeve let her hair down and shook it out. "I'm just glad I was able to help."

"Who did you know how to find that Balladyn didn't?"

She closed her eyes with her back still turned to Leon. He just had to ask that question. Why couldn't he have left well enough alone?

Maeve turned to him and wrinkled her nose. "The king asked that I keep the information to myself."

"Oh, of course," Leon hurried to say. Then he grinned. "I like the idea of him coming to you for help, though. That means he owes you now. And that's always a good thing."

Maeve smiled and nodded. "Yes. Yes, it is."

"I thought you might want to know that your party was a success."

"See? I keep telling you that it goes great without me there."

"But it's your party," Leon said as he pushed away from the doorframe. "They need to see you to be reminded of that. And speaking of being reminded, there is an issue with a couple of employees."

This was the part Maeve hated about what she did. She steeled herself and asked, "What happened?"

"They stole from you. Most of the money is gone, but we managed to retrieve some of it."

Stealing was sometimes the start of something more. Maeve had to put an end to this—and make an example of those who dared to steal from her.

Yet . . . she didn't want to do anything to the employees. It was a weakness to let their daring go unpunished, but she just couldn't bring herself to do it. Not this time. "Is that all?"

Leon's eyes bugged out. "Is that all? That's enough to have both of them executed."

"I know. I'm waiting to hear all of their crimes."

"Maeve, you can't waffle now."

"I'm not." But both of them knew it was a lie.

Leon advanced on her and lowered his voice. "I know you don't like handing down sentences, but it's what got you to this position. That's why you're so feared. It's been a while since you've ordered a death. It's time. Because if you don't, then everyone will begin stealing from you. Before you know it, this empire you've built will be gone."

"I don't want to lose anything."

"Then you know what to do."

She released a long breath, her heart aching at what she had to do. "My rule is that anyone who steals from me must die."

Leon wrapped an arm around her and pulled her against him for a hug. "There's no other way."

"I knew what I was getting into all those eons ago," she said. "I knew that it would be hard."

She just hadn't realized that it would never get easier. In fact, it only became more difficult. But the Dark were scavengers. The minute one of them saw a weakness, they swooped in. And it didn't take long for others to follow.

Leon leaned back and searched her face. "You're different somehow. I can't put my finger on how."

She would never tell him that she'd visited the Light Castle. It didn't matter that she had been there all of a couple of minutes, it'd left a lasting impression on her. So had Bradach, for that matter.

"I'm still me," Maeve told Leon with a forced smile. "We carry out the punishment tomorrow."

Leon nodded. "You don't have to be there."

"Yes, I do. You know that as well as I. I have to look these Fae in the eye and give them their sentence."

Her longtime friend lifted a lock of her hair. "You've never once laid a hand on a single person, and yet you have the silver in your hair like all other Dark."

"I may not be killing people directly, but it's by my hand that it's happening."

Leon gave her a kiss on the forehead. "Rest. I'll see you in the morning."

Maeve didn't move until she heard the door to her chamber close. Then she made sure Leon had gone before she put up the spells to keep her doors and windows locked. No one would be able to get into her chambers. Not even by teleporting.

Only then did she walk to the bathroom and look in the mirror. She dropped the glamour that had become like a second skin to her. Silver eyes stared back at her, but the silver in her hair remained.

She was neither Dark nor Light. She didn't fit in either world. Her father had helped to hide her lack of red eyes and the missing silver in her black hair for as long as he'd been alive. She would never forget the day he'd come to her and told her that he was tired of everything.

It was a weakness one of his enemies saw. They took aim. The next day, her father was found murdered in his office.

Maeve didn't think twice about taking over the company. She, along with Leon and some of her father's dedicated people, had tracked down who had murdered him. Using glamour around others had become second nature, so no one knew that she'd never harmed a single individual.

Not until she ordered the Fae's death.

That evening when she was alone, she'd dropped her glamour and discovered the first glimpse of silver in her hair. And it had continued like that ever since.

No one knew her secret but Leon. And no one ever would. Every one of her clients would shun her, and she would be left with nothing. All because she'd never taken a life.

Maeve removed the rest of her clothes and crawled naked into bed. As she slid between the sheets, she rolled onto her side and thought of Bradach. Had he succeeded in getting Xaneth free of Usaeil?

She hadn't heard anything about the queen being toppled, and that worried her. Because that meant there was a good chance that Bradach had failed.

Maeve bit her lip to keep from saying Bradach's name, calling him to her. It wasn't as if she would know what to say if he were there anyway. She doubted he'd take kindly to her telling him that she just wanted to know what it was like to kiss him.

Her eyes closed as her thoughts remained on Bradach. All the while wondering if she'd ever see him again.

CHAPTER
eleven

No matter how much Bradach wanted to storm the estate and find Xaneth himself, he knew he couldn't. Usaeil was too smart for such tactics. And the one thing Bradach wasn't, was reckless. He'd been veiled from the moment Maeve had left.

"Eoghan," he said, his voice traveling on the wind.

Seconds later, the Reaper leader arrived, also veiled. Eoghan's quicksilver gaze met Bradach's before he looked around to get his bearings. "I take this to mean you've found Xaneth."

Bradach ran a hand over his chin. "Not exactly."

"I don't see Maeve."

"I sent her home."

"I see. Why don't you tell me what happened?"

Bradach relayed details of the time he'd been with Maeve after Balladyn had introduced them, though he left out the fact that she'd seen him remain veiled.

Eoghan eyed him for a full minute in silence. "You took Maeve to the Light Castle?"

"She needed to be convinced about Usaeil."

"I was right in believing you could carry out this mission. Not only did you work well with Balladyn, but you also won over Maeve, which we all knew wouldn't be easy."

Bradach wasn't comfortable taking full credit for that. "It was Balladyn asking for a favor that got me in. Maeve said as much."

"Regardless, you sealed the deal."

"Just because Usaeil is down there doesn't mean Xaneth is," he pointed out.

Eoghan grunted and faced the large mansion. "Had the queen not imparted this location to Maeve, we likely would not have found her. Usaeil's magic is stronger than any of us realized."

"Cael would have found Usaeil. Eventually."

Eoghan issued another grunt, this one softer. "Cael is learning his new abilities quickly, but this was the faster option."

"No, the most efficient way would have been for Death to judge Usaeil so she could locate the queen and we could reap Usaeil's soul."

Quicksilver eyes slowly turned to Bradach. Eoghan said in a calm voice, "And you know why Erith won't do that."

"Because it's Rhi's destiny to kill the queen." Bradach shook his head in irritation. "That's shite. Death has said many times that she can't see the future. How does she know?"

"How does Death know anything?" Eoghan replied. "As far as I know, her powers are untapped. I knew she wasn't a Fae. And after the battle with Bran, I'm beginning to think that Erith is, in fact, a goddess."

"Which makes Cael a god now since he has some of her powers?"

Eoghan shrugged and crossed his arms over his chest. "I don't know, and I don't care. Death gave us a mission. I chose you to carry it out. It doesn't matter what reason Erith has for why Rhi has to be the one to take down Usaeil. And we aren't here to question that. We're Reapers. We serve Death."

"I just don't want Usaeil to turn into another Bran. Erith had a chance to kill him once."

"And you believe that since she has a chance to judge Usaeil, that Death is making a similar mistake in allowing Rhi to be the one to take the queen down?"

Hadn't he just said as much? But Bradach kept the question to himself. Instead, he nodded once.

Eoghan sighed and dropped his arms to his sides. "Erith won't make the same mistake twice. I am interested in the Trackers. Let's go for a closer look."

"Wait," Bradach said just as Eoghan was about to walk away.

"What is it?" Eoghan asked, concern clouding his face.

Bradach glanced at the house. "I don't know exactly. Just . . . a feeling."

"My instincts have saved me more times than I can count. What are yours telling you?"

"That the queen knows we're here. I don't know how, but she does."

"A spell around the estate perhaps? Like what Bran used?"

Bradach shook his head. "I felt nothing like that. Besides, when I came face-to-face with two of the Trackers, she had the opportunity to trap me if she wanted."

"Maybe it was simply to allow her to know when someone breached it."

"There was nothing." Bradach thought back to when he'd caught a glimpse of the queen. "Usaeil looked directly at this slope. She didn't see me or Maeve, but there was no denying in which direction Usaeil focused her gaze."

Eoghan nodded as he listened. "The Tracker might have sensed something that he didn't let you know about."

"Usaeil must realize that we'd come for Xaneth."

"That's a possibility I've thought of, as well," Eoghan admitted. "Which poses a problem."

"Especially now. If she suspects someone is here, then she'll guess it's us."

"Exactly." Eoghan's liquid silver gaze focused on the house as he carefully looked it over. "I could call the rest of the Reapers. The seven of us could storm the residence."

When he didn't continue, Bradach asked, "But?"

"You're right. Something is wrong. It's like she wants us to do that."

Bradach made a sound in the back of his throat. "Usaeil isn't threatened by us. She's taunting us."

"That's a big mistake."

"But she's right. Death didn't judge her, and we didn't go after Usaeil when she ran from the castle after believing that she'd killed Thea."

Eoghan's head swiveled to Bradach, a smile playing on the leader's lips. "Usaeil's overconfidence can work to our advantage."

"We have to fight her and free Xaneth, all without killing her. That might prove . . . difficult."

"It's what has been deemed."

Bradach considered Eoghan's words as he tried to think up a plan. Then it hit him. "We need to get in the house. Why not have one of us draw Usaeil away?"

"She doesn't seem the type to leave her fortress. There is only one person who could get her to leave."

Bradach huffed. "Do you really think Constantine would do that since he and Rhi are gearing up to take down Usaeil?"

"We won't know until we ask," Eoghan stated. "Besides, it might be just what the Dragon Kings and Rhi need to get them to attack."

Bradach wished he'd thought of it himself. "I like that idea. Have them attack Usaeil while we free Xaneth. Sounds good to me. Let's go to Dreagan."

Eoghan was smiling when he reached over and grasped Bradach's arm. In the next second, they stood outside Dreagan Manor in Scotland.

Both lowered their veil at the same time. They made their way to the entrance, but it was Eoghan who knocked. A pretty woman with long, straight, ginger-colored hair and light blue eyes opened the door.

"Can I help you?" she asked in a perfect Scots accent.

They had no time to reply as a man came up behind her. The moment his gaze met theirs, he carefully moved the woman behind him. "Gentlemen."

"You know us?" Bradach asked.

Eoghan leaned his head over and said, "They have a force field around all of Dreagan. They get notified of anyone who passes through it."

So that was the zing of magic Bradach had felt before they materialized. He'd thought it was just Eoghan's teleportation.

Eoghan then turned his attention to the Dragon King. "We're Reapers. I'm Eoghan, and this is Bradach. We'd like to speak with Constantine."

The Dragon King relaxed a fraction. "We've had a few dealings with Reapers, but I've not seen either of you. I'm Cináed, and this is my mate, Gemma," he said of the woman. Then he sighed. "You won't be able to talk to Con, though."

"It won't take long," Bradach said. "We've located Usaeil, and we were hoping he might wish to help."

Cináed's gray eyes widened. "You know where that bitch is?"

"Let us talk with Con," Eoghan urged. "We'll tell you everything."

"I'd bring you to him right now if I could," Cináed said. "But Usaeil took him."

Now that wasn't something Bradach had expected to hear. He and Eoghan exchanged looks. Then he told Cináed, "It looks like we might be able to help each other then."

The King swung open the door. "Come in. I'll get the others."

Cináed walked away, leaving Gemma to show Eoghan and Bradach into a front sitting room that was larger than any Bradach had ever seen.

"Can I get you anything?" Gemma asked.

Eoghan smiled. "That's kind, but we're fine."

Worry reflected in Gemma's eyes. "I'm glad you came. Maybe now the Kings will be able to locate Con."

Then she turned and left. They didn't have long to wait before a handful of Dragon Kings walked into the room. Bradach had seen some of them from a distance. The only one he'd ever spoken with was Con, so he was excited to meet more of them.

The first one gave a nod of his head, his long, black hair pulled into a queue behind his neck. His gold eyes were like lasers as they shifted from Bradach to Eoghan. "I'm Ulrik. Cináed says you've located Usaeil."

"We have," Eoghan answered.

"Where?" asked another King, this one had wavy, caramel-colored hair that fell just past his shoulders, and celadon eyes.

It was Ulrik who said, "That's Kellan. The others are Rhys, V, Keltan, and Sebastian."

"I'm Bradach, and this is Eoghan, the leader of my group of Reapers," he explained.

The anger and frustration rolling off the Dragon Kings came in waves akin to a storm battering cliffs. Bradach understood a little of what they were going through. While he hadn't known Eoghan when he disappeared from Bran's magic, he had been a Reaper—and that had hit all of them hard.

"Where is she?" Ulrik demanded.

It was Eoghan who said, "She's taken a friend of ours, as well. We're hoping to use Con to lure her out so we can get into her estate and find Xaneth."

"Why not just attack her?" the King with the ice blue eyes asked.

"V has a point," Ulrik said. "We know how powerful the Reapers are. You don't need us for that."

Bradach shook his head. "No, we don't. If Death had judged the queen and we were going to reap her soul. But Death hasn't done that because she's waiting on Rhi."

"Fuck me," said the King with aqua-ringed dark blue eyes.

Bradach didn't like the looks passing over the faces of the Kings.

Eoghan asked, "Is Rhi here?"

Ulrik shook his head. "Rhi has been . . . difficult to get ahold of lately."

"Has something happened to her?" Bradach asked.

Rhys said, "Nay, she's alive. She's just coming to terms with what has been going on."

Bradach raised a brow. "What aren't you telling us?"

It was V who said, "Ulrik and I spoke to Usaeil. She used glamour."

"So?" Bradach said with a shrug. Lots of Fae used glamour.

But Eoghan frowned at the Kings. "You say that as if you're surprised."

"We can see through glamour," Ulrik said.

V crossed his thick arms over his chest. "We believed we spoke with Inen."

"Captain of the Queen's Guard," Bradach said. "We know him."

"Except we were no' speaking with him," Ulrik stated. "Turns out, it was Usaeil using glamour."

V's blue eyes turned even icier. "She tricked us into giving her information about how Rhi trusted Inen, and that we would, as well."

"Fek me, is right," Bradach said and ran a hand down his face.

Ulrik's gold eyes moved between them once more. "How did you find the queen?"

"She mentioned something to an acquaintance," Bradach explained. "Balladyn introduced me to this Dark, Maeve, who gave me information on the city. From there, we searched until we found the right place."

V dropped his arms and stepped forward. "And you saw her? Usaeil?"

Bradach nodded.

"Take us there," Ulrik commanded.

"Y ou can let go of me now," V stated with a raised brow.

Bradach rolled his eyes but didn't release his hold on the Dragon King's arm. "Trust me, I'd rather not be touching you."

"He has to, V," Ulrik said. "They're veiled, and as long as they're touching us, we're veiled, as well."

V issued an exaggerated sigh. "How could I forget?"

Bradach looked toward Eoghan.

His leader grinned and mouthed, "Can you imagine if Rordan were here?"

Bradach swallowed a chuckle at the thought of the Reaper who always had a smartass comment at the ready.

V's eyes narrowed when he caught Bradach and Eoghan sharing a smile, but the King didn't comment on it. Thank the stars.

Bradach didn't have much thought on the Dragon Kings. They took their positions as guardians of the realm seriously. He'd been too young during the Fae Wars to take part, but he'd heard enough tales about the way the dragons had fought.

Despite his lack of hate or affinity, the simple fact was that the Reapers needed the Kings. Though, it now looked as if the Reapers would be the ones helping the dragons out.

"Where did you see her?" Ulrik asked.

Bradach looked toward the King of Silvers. While he might not have many feelings about the Dragon Kings, he knew of them. Especially Ulrik, who, up until recently, had been banished from Dreagan. Now, after finding his place with his kin again, and with Con gone, Ulrik had clearly taken over as leader.

If he didn't know any better, Bradach might think that Ulrik had been a part of it all to get rid of Constantine. But the simple truth was that the Kings were nobler than that. If Ulrik had wanted to be King of Dragon Kings, he would've fought Con for the position.

Bradach pointed to the back of the house. "There."

"And she looked here?" V asked.

Bradach nodded. "She couldn't see me, but yes. She looked in this direction."

"Since this slope offers a view of the back of her estate, it seems logical that she would direct her gaze here," Eoghan pointed out.

Ulrik eyed the house for a moment before looking at Eoghan and then Bradach. "So, Usaeil thinks someone is here. But is it the Reapers or the Kings?"

"Or Rhi?" V pointed out.

Bradach lifted one shoulder in a shrug. "If Usaeil has any kind of intelligence, she'll make sure that she's prepared for any and all of us."

"Including us working together?" Ulrik queried. "She knows we would help Rhi."

Eoghan's quicksilver eyes met Ulrik's. "There's a chance she'll think we've teamed up. After all, Con did help the Reapers with Thea."

"I doona care how strong Usaeil believes she is, she can no' stand against all of us," V pointed out.

Bradach glanced at the King of Coppers. "I agree with him."

"Usaeil can no' stand against the Kings nor the Reapers alone. But Rhi?" Ulrik said. "That's another matter entirely."

V's forehead furrowed. "Rhi willna attack the queen on her own."

"That's why Rhi came to Con," Ulrik said.

Eoghan nodded. "As much as I believe that Rhi has untapped magic within her, I think she realizes she needs the Kings with her."

"What if Rhi does go after Usaeil on her own?" Three pairs of eyes turned to Bradach. "Think about it. The queen will be looking for Reapers and Kings. She won't be keeping watch for one Fae."

Ulrik shook his head slowly. "Rhi can no' die."

It was something about the way the King said it that got Bradach's attention. "I'm not saying she would."

"But there's a good chance of that if Rhi faces Usaeil on her own," V said. "Besides, Balladyn already said he would be with Rhi when she went after Usaeil."

Bradach's eyes widened as he looked to Eoghan. How had neither of them known that? Because they'd been so intent on their own mission that they hadn't been thinking about anything —or anyone—else.

"If that's true, then Usaeil is prepared for an army, because Balladyn will have his with him," Eoghan stated.

Bradach raised his brows. "I repeat again, an army versus one."

V cut his gaze to Bradach and pointed toward one of the Trackers patrolling the area. "Are you forgetting those?"

"None of this matters," Ulrik stated in a sharp tone. "Usaeil willna have her battle here. It'll be in Ireland close to the Light Castle so all her people can see."

"You mean so they'll see Rhi, the Reapers, Dragon Kings, and Balladyn coming at them," Eoghan said.

"Doona forget the Dark army," V added.

Bradach laughed dryly. "Usaeil doesn't stand a chance against all of us."

Eoghan glanced at the ground before he looked at Bradach. "But the Light will see it as everyone attacking them. No matter what any of us say, they'll believe whatever Usaeil tells them. And they will fight with her."

Bradach twisted his lips. "Then we should do this now. The four of us go in. We find Xaneth and Con and get out."

"You're assuming they're in there," V said.

Eoghan looked at them, his gaze stopping on Bradach. "I have an idea."

"And that is?" Bradach asked.

"Go back to Maeve. The two of you return to the Light Castle and begin telling the others who Usaeil really is. It won't take long for the gossip to spread."

Ulrik frowned as he shrugged. "Why? Just to keep some of the Light from fighting with Usaeil?"

"That's part of it, yes," Eoghan said. "But also because it's not something Usaeil will have thought of. She'll assume all of us will stay out of the castle as we plan for war."

V suddenly smiled. "As soon as Usaeil hears the whispers,

because she will, she'll return to find out who started it and put an end to them."

"Exactly," Eoghan said with a wide grin.

One side of Ulrik's mouth lifted in a smile. "It would get her out of the house here so we can go inside and look for Xaneth and Con."

Bradach very much wanted to be a part of the fight, but he would come in toward the end. Really, he just wanted a shot at the Trackers. The fekkers were just . . . wrong.

And yet, there was a tingle of excitement in his stomach at the idea of seeing Maeve again. If he hadn't thoroughly pissed her off enough that she refused to see him. Even if he had, he would convince her to help him. Simply because he couldn't imagine anyone else by his side.

"I'll head to Maeve's then," Bradach said.

He waited until Eoghan had shifted and now had a hand on both Dragon Kings before he teleported to Maeve's mansion. When he arrived, it was night. Lights were on outside the grand house, but everything felt oddly quiet. Disconnected somehow.

Bradach raised his veil and made his way around the residence, noting there wasn't a single guard. When he reached the back, he stopped, and his gaze immediately lifted to the top floor where he knew Maeve's rooms were.

The lights were out. But that's not what bothered him. It was the eerie silence. He knew the sound well.

It was the sound of death.

Bradach chose not to teleport inside. Instead, he cautiously walked to the back door so he could search room by room. Halfway to the entrance, he saw that the door wasn't quite closed. He paused once more and listened, hoping to hear something. But there was nothing.

He slowly pushed open the door wide enough to step through. Light illuminated the back room and preceding hallways. Yet he knew in his gut that something was dreadfully wrong. Maeve was too smart to not have the house locked and guards on patrol. Not to mention magic around her home to alert her if anyone attacked.

Bradach slowly made his way through the house. He didn't find a single person in any of the rooms. There was no blood or bodies either. The only sign that something was wrong—besides the silence—was the open back door and a candleholder that was on its side.

He opted not to check the rest of the lower level before finding out if Maeve was all right. At the base of the curving stairs, he looked up but didn't see anyone. Bradach teleported to the top of the staircase and looked down the empty corridor.

Then he started toward Maeve's chambers. The hallway lights were dimmed, casting shadows everywhere. He cautiously walked down the passage. He'd only taken a few steps when he heard a soft humph.

Alarm went through him at the thought of Maeve being hurt. He teleported right inside her chambers to see it in total disarray. His head snapped to the side when he heard a crash and a growl— one he recognized.

Trackers.

He rushed toward the sound. As he entered through a door hanging by one hinge, he skidded to a halt in the dark room when he saw a petite form kneeling over a prone Tracker.

Maeve jerked up her head, her black and silver hair flying back as she searched the area. He dropped his veil, and her gaze landed on him. She slowly straightened, yanking a weapon from the Tracker's chest. Bradach saw the black tank top and skimpy black panties she wore were as coated with blood as her face and body.

In her hand was a dagger with a long, thick, curving blade that dripped with the blood of the Tracker.

"Maeve?" he called tentatively.

She didn't move, remaining just out of the moonlight that bathed the floor, streaming through one of the many windows.

"Are you hurt?" he asked as he took a few slow steps toward her.

After a moment, she swallowed and shook her head. "I couldn't sleep. It was the only reason I saw it. It was so . . . silent. It didn't make a single sound."

He reached her in another few steps. He'd had a sister and knew when a female needed to be comforted, but he was hesitant to offer that to Maeve.

Then she lifted her eyes to him, and he saw the silver shade. This wasn't glamour. And yet her hair still had silver in it. He didn't understand, but frankly, it didn't matter.

"You're alive," he told her.

"It was fast, Bradach. So very fast."

He saw her hand tremble then, and without another thought, he pulled her into his arms. For a second, she remained stiff. Then with a soft exhale, she relaxed and wound her arms around him.

"You killed it," he told her, stroking her back.

She said nothing, just stood in his arms and let him hold her. He liked her there. He rested his cheek atop her head and looked down at the Tracker. He didn't know why it hadn't faded to ash and drifted away. Perhaps it had something to do with the fact that it wasn't Light or Dark anymore but something else altogether.

He didn't know how much time had passed before Maeve stepped out of his arms and met his gaze. "What are you doing here?"

"I came to see if you wanted to help me again."

She pointed to the Tracker without looking at it. "Usaeil sent that. She knows I assisted you."

"She couldn't. She never saw you."

"And yet that thing entered my home," she stated loudly, anger contorting her face. "It got through my wards around the grounds and house. I'm guessing since no one came up here to see what the commotion was about that they're all dead?"

Bradach gave a single shake of his head. "I didn't search everywhere. The few rooms I saw were empty."

"Leon," she said and rushed past Bradach.

"Maeve. Wait," he called. But it was too late. She'd already teleported away.

Bradach followed the trail of her magic from one room to the next, floor to floor as they found absolutely nothing. Not a single person remained.

Finally, she stopped in the ballroom he'd been in the night before. She looked dazed, worry and shock causing her skin to pale. "I can't find Leon."

"Could he have run off?" Bradach asked.

Had it only been a few hours since the party? It felt like days.

She shook her head. "Leon would never have willingly left me. I don't know how the Trackers kill."

"I need to get the body to someone who can study it," Bradach told her. "For some reason, it hasn't disintegrated."

Maeve turned her head to him. "What are you waiting for? Go."

"I'm not leaving you. Another could return."

"You want to bring me with you?" she asked, a brow raised in doubt.

Fek. He couldn't do that. There had to be another option. Then he realized what it was. "We're going back to the Light Castle."

"Why?"

"To hurt Usaeil. Want to come?"

"Yes," she said and snapped her fingers. Her hair changed to all black, while the blood disappeared, and a bright pink dress covered her. "I need to find Leon."

When she turned away to take another look around for Leon, Bradach called for Eoghan. The Reaper appeared immediately with both Ulrik and V still veiled. Bradach pointed upstairs and mouthed, "Hurry."

Then he turned to Maeve and held out his hand.

thirteen

The traitorous bitch. Usaeil should've known. But of all the people to betray her, she hadn't thought the first in line would be Maeve the Merciless.

Usaeil stared out the upper floor window of the ruins of the Light Castle on the Fae Realm, her arms crossed as she thought about Maeve. The ruthless Dark that had built her empire on the ashes of her father's death was someone Usaeil had kept her eye on for a long time. She'd watched as Maeve clawed her way to the top, toppling over anyone who got in her way.

To think, Usaeil had considered Maeve someone she might bring into her new court as an ally. It just proved to Usaeil that there was no one she could trust other than herself. Everyone was out to get her.

But Maeve? Why her? Why now?

Usaeil's gaze narrowed. Her mind immediately went to Rhi. Then she laughed. Rhi was a great many things, and she might dirty herself to interact with Balladyn because they were old friends, but that's where things ended. There was no way Rhi would have searched out Maeve.

Besides, Rhi had no inkling about those Usaeil dealt with.

That the Dragon Kings were involved was a good possibility. No matter how much she tried, Usaeil had yet to curtail their magic. Despite the years and the growth of her power, she couldn't match theirs without a little help—namely that of the Druids.

But the Kings hated the Dark Fae. There was absolutely no way they would ever work with one.

That left only two other enemies: Balladyn and the Reapers.

While Balladyn had managed to do a great many good deeds for the Dark since he took the throne, he wasn't smart enough to piece together the intricate network of Fae Usaeil had cultivated through the eons.

Not alone, at least.

The Reapers were a different story, however. They weren't strong enough to bring her down, but that didn't mean they wouldn't try to irritate her. Which is exactly what they were doing. It really was too bad that they had brought Maeve into it.

Usaeil didn't care how they had gotten the Dark to help them. She didn't even concern herself with how they had figured out that she'd had dealings with Maeve in the past. It was enough that the Dark female had imparted to them the one thing Usaeil had told her—the location of one of her secret places.

The divulging of such a confidential piece of information had been done on purpose. Usaeil had told the four Fae she'd considered for positions in her new court four different locations to see if any—or all-would betray her.

It galled her that it was Maeve. Out of the four, she'd honestly believed that Maeve would hold out the longest. But the Dark would no longer be a problem once the Tracker was finished with her.

Usaeil had Trackers at all of the locations to make it appear as if she were there. It'd worked for the Napa house. But the more Usaeil thought about Maeve turning on her, the angrier she became. She'd had plans for the Dark.

Maeve had the makings of a truly great Fae. But she'd been turned.

By Reapers.

Maybe Usaeil should've remained with Bran to fight the Reapers. Together, the two of them could've easily wiped them out. Death and her Reapers were a thorn in Usaeil's side that she wanted gone. She wasn't exactly afraid to fight them. Because to admit to any kind of fear, even to herself, was to permit an enemy to get into her head. And Usaeil simply couldn't allow that to happen.

It was one of the reasons she'd managed to stay queen for so long.

She'd been terrified of Death and the Reapers once. Now that she knew the truth of them, they were much less frightening. It angered her that she'd allowed the legends and tales of the Reapers to cause her to react in such a way.

If only she'd remained behind after killing Thea, she could've rid herself of the Reapers and Death. That would've helped Bran, though.

Just thinking about Bran made her grimace. She'd thought he would be a good partner, but in truth, all he wanted was to take Death's place. Except he would've taken over the realm. She'd realized that the moment he refused to acknowledge her as his queen.

It also sealed his fate, because she'd known then that she would do anything in her power to make sure he didn't win that battle with Death. In the end, Usaeil hadn't had to do much of anything. Bran had outplayed his hand. It was a mistake she wouldn't make.

But that still left the Reapers to deal with. Usaeil's Trackers were strong, but not nearly strong enough against the Reapers. She didn't want to lose any of her secret army. They had begun as a way to disappear those she wanted gone, but it hadn't taken Usaeil long to realize just how important the Trackers were.

The fact that both the Light and Dark moved from place to place, never remaining too long in one location, made it easy for her to find the ones she wanted. Some she took, but others she easily lured to her.

The thrill of becoming something . . . more . . . was something no Fae could resist. It didn't matter if they were Light or Dark, they always sought more power, more magic. More everything.

Usaeil let her eyes move away from the one window in the entire castle that hadn't been shattered, broken, or demolished. Every time she looked out of it, she could almost believe that the stronghold was intact.

Almost.

But the wasteland of the Fae Realm on the other side of the pane was proof that it was all an illusion.

Life had been perfect here. Had the civil war not destroyed the planet, she would've never met the Druids. Or gone to Earth. It was there that she'd caught sight of her first dragon.

His gold scales had sparkled brightly in the sun. He flew alone, surveying his domain with a watchful, commanding eye. He'd been huge and utterly magnificent. The way he moved gracefully in the air, the whoosh of his enormous wings, and his roar. Even now remembering the sound of it sent chills racing over Usaeil's skin.

She'd known then that he was the one who ruled them. The one who wielded the most power. It meant that he was a threat. One that had to be removed.

Yet that had proven more difficult than either she or the Druids had expected. Then they'd gotten a glimpse of the dragons' magic. It had made Usaeil want to run as far and as fast from the dragon realm as she could.

But she held fast when the Druids' gazes locked on her. She realized then that they'd known exactly how powerful the dragons were. Before she could even ask why they'd brought her to such a world, they laid out their plan.

It was one that required patience, but it would also give Usaeil everything she'd ever dreamed of.

She closed her eyes. How silly she'd been to think that. Her dreams had changed through the years, just as she had. She'd kept them to herself, however. There was no need to alert the Druids.

Not yet, at least.

That was for another time.

It wasn't as if she were scared of the Druids. It was more that she dreaded what they would do in retaliation. Usaeil couldn't take them all on. They were much more powerful than the poor excuses for Druids on Earth. No, these Druids were mighty in strength and in numbers. Yet, for all their magic, even they couldn't bring down a single Dragon King on their own.

They needed the Fae just as much as the Fae needed them. That was the only reason they hadn't betrayed one another.

Usaeil turned on her heel and walked through what was left of her bedchamber. She stepped over broken stone while her feet crunched on glass as she made her way through the ruins until she came to the doorway that she'd created that led back to Earth.

A sound behind her made her stop. She pivoted, her eyes

searching. Someone or something was on the realm. It had been dead and forgotten for a long time now. She was the only one who returned, which is how she knew that there wasn't anything left living on the plane.

She waited, her gaze searching for any movements. Then Usaeil sent out a blast of magic meant to reveal. There was a gasp when her magic landed in a corner. In the next heartbeat, Moreann appeared.

"Spying on me?" Usaeil demanded of the Druid empress.

Moreann's green eyes held Usaeil's. "You're keeping something from me."

"You keep a great deal from me, and yet I don't spy on you."

The empress held her ground. "We made a pact, Usaeil. It can't be broken."

"You say that as if I wasn't there. I'm painfully aware of the magic that binds us."

"Sometimes I wonder."

Usaeil fought the anger that rose up like a fast-moving tide within her. "Don't."

"I know just how ambitious you are," Moreann said with a lift of her chin. "I used that in order to convince you to join me."

"Does it matter why I joined?"

"You know it does. Especially to me. I knew there would come a day when you tried to get out of our pact."

Usaeil snorted and shook her head. "I'm not trying to get out of anything. You have your plans. I have mine."

"And just what are your plans?" Moreann demanded.

Usaeil smiled. "The same as I've said from day one. I'm going to rule the entire Fae, not just the Light."

Moreann stared at Usaeil for a long moment. "Hmm. I believe that, but I know you well enough to know that you have something else up your sleeve."

"As long as it doesn't interfere with our pact, what does it matter?"

"Don't deceive me, Usaeil. Fae queen or not, you won't like my retribution."

Usaeil closed the distance between them until only a few inches separated them. "Remember who came to who, Moreann. You want something, but you need the Fae. If you want to succeed, don't piss me off." She started to turn away then stopped and swung her gaze back to the empress. "And let me make myself perfectly clear. If you try to get in my way, if you try to thwart any of my plans that have nothing to do with our pact, I will destroy you."

"You'll try," Moreann stated with a raised brow.

Usaeil narrowed her eyes. "I'll succeed."

With a snap of her fingers, Moreann vanished. Usaeil hated that the Druid had been in the castle. It was her own fault, though. She'd been the one to suggest they hold their meetings here since no one would see them.

Now, it felt as if Moreann were intruding on something. But to move their meeting place would raise suspicions. The fact that the empress was there on a day when a gathering between them hadn't been scheduled was cause for concern.

It meant that Moreann was watching her, waiting to find something. Not that the Druid would. Usaeil was too good for that, but she still didn't like it.

Usaeil cast a spell around the ruins of the castle and a hundred meters beyond, that would alert her when and if any Druids showed up again. Whether it was for their regular meetings or not, she wanted to be prepared.

She returned to the Fae doorway and stepped through it, expecting to see the Tracker she'd sent after Maeve. The fact that it wasn't there could mean any number of things. Maybe Maeve was proving to be better at evading the Tracker than Usaeil had expected.

The one thing Usaeil knew for certain was that Maeve would never be able to defeat one of her army.

CHAPTER
fourteen

"**W**hat the holy fuck is that thing?" V asked as he stared down at the creature.

Eoghan squatted beside the Tracker, turning his head one way and then the other as he looked it over. "Usaeil's creation."

"This reminds me of the wee beasts Deirdre created," Ulrik said. "The wyrran."

Eoghan's head snapped up to the King of Silvers. "Deirdre?"

"She was a Druid," Ulrik explained. "A drough intent on commanding the Warriors."

V crossed his arms over his chest as he curled his lip at the Tracker. "Did the wyrran look like this?"

Ulrik shook his head of black hair. "No' at all, but the comparisons of both women in power creating creatures that answer only to them is a wee bit too close to the mark for me."

"Is this drough dead?" Eoghan asked.

"Oh, aye," Ulrik said with raised brows. "The Warriors and Druids of MacLeod Castle made sure of that."

V grunted. "There's that, at least."

"And the wyrran?" Eoghan was more than concerned at the sight of the Trackers. He'd had no idea that Usaeil had done such a thing.

Ulrik gave a single shake of his head. "Gone, as well."

Eoghan got to his feet and stared down with distaste at the Tracker. "It's Fae. A Light Fae previously."

"Does it matter if it's Light or Dark?" V asked.

"Usaeil is Dark herself now," Ulrik pointed out.

Eoghan ran a hand down his face. "Everyone who intends to fight against Usaeil needs to know about the Trackers. They can be killed. And thanks to Bradach, we know they have a heightened sense of smell and hearing."

Ulrik's lips twisted. "They're like dogs."

"Nothing can withstand dragon fire," V said with a smirk.

But Eoghan wasn't thinking of the Dragon Kings battling the Trackers. He was thinking of Rhi. All Fae, really. The Trackers might have enhanced senses, but they would be no match for a Reaper. Bradach had already discovered that.

But Rhi? Balladyn? Or other Fae?

"What are you thinking?" Ulrik asked.

Eoghan swung his gaze to the two Dragon Kings. "That we made a mistake in underestimating Usaeil. Everyone has."

V's lips twisted in anger. "That we have. There's still time to correct things."

"Is there?" Ulrik asked. "She has Con."

"And Xaneth," Eoghan interjected.

Ulrik glanced at him and nodded. "I thought Usaeil's plan was simple. Take Con and keep him until he does what she wants."

"Which is for him to make her his mate." V shivered, his face filled with disgust.

Eoghan raised a brow. "You think it might be more than that?"

"I'm no' entirely convinced she's holding Con," Ulrik replied. "I think there's a really good chance that he's allowing her to believe that so he can find out just what kind of crazy she is."

V blew out a breath. "I can no' help but agree. Con isna King of Dragon Kings for nothing. He's powerful in both strength and magic. I doona care what Usaeil has done, she wouldna be able to hold him."

Eoghan hoped to hell that they were right. Because if Usaeil were able to contain a Dragon King, then their problems had gotten significantly bigger. "The issue is that we won't know until we can see Con. But I'm not sure we can find him if we can't even locate Xaneth."

"He's probably dead," V stated.

Ulrik, however, shook his head. "Or turned into a Tracker."

Eoghan didn't even want to think about that. Unfortunately, he had no other choice. The simple fact was that there was a good chance that Usaeil had decided not to kill her nephew and had turned him into something she could use. Another cog in her army.

"Fek," he murmured.

V dropped his arms to his sides. "Usaeil isna just your problem, Eoghan. She's ours, as well. Especially now that she's seen fit to kidnap Con."

"This is bigger than just the Dragon Kings and the Reapers," Ulrik said.

Eoghan's eyes narrowed. "How so?"

"The Others."

V mumbled something beneath his breath as he turned away.

He walked a few steps before he returned to them, looking more perturbed than before.

Eoghan raised a brow at Ulrik, waiting for the King to continue.

Ulrik released a long breath. "The Others are Druids and Fae, both good and bad, Light and Dark, who have joined together to combine their magic to take down the Dragon Kings."

Eoghan blinked, hoping he was joking. But it soon became apparent they were anything but. "How do you know this?"

"A small wooden dragon found on Fair Isle beneath the skeleton of a White. The wooden dragon was an exact replica of Con. And to make matters worse, each time a human touched it, they wanted to kill us."

Eoghan swallowed. "And if a King touched it?"

V's lips flattened. "We want to kill humans."

"What about a Fae?" Eoghan asked.

Ulrik widened his stance. "Shara briefly laid her hands on it and was struck unconscious. It was Rhi who was able to get the object contained in a field of her power that then allowed her to pick up the mie, drough, Light Fae, and Dark Fae magic."

"That's no' all," V said. "The Others tried to steal my sword."

Eoghan shrugged, not seeing how important one Dragon King's sword was over another.

"V's sword can check on our dragons and see how they are," Ulrik explained. "He can also call them home with it."

And just when Eoghan thought that might be it, V continued.

"It took me and Roman, along with two gypsies from Romania who were descendants of a group of humans I protected eons ago, to discover where my sword has been all these millennia. Iceland."

Eoghan shook his head in confusion. "Wait. I thought you said they tried to steal your sword."

"They did try. One of the humans I protected foresaw what the Others intended and had men take it from me before the Others could get to it. The Others got into my head and wiped all my memories of the entire episode."

Ulrik sighed. "Needless to say, V has his sword returned, but the Others made him work for it. They set traps for both V and Roman, but V was able to dismantle the magic they used in his mind and unlock all his memories."

V glanced away. "In the mountain in Iceland, we found two massive walls of rock. There was writing on each. One had what I believe is Druid writing. The other was Fae. Rhi was there. She saw it."

"How does that connect to Usaeil?" Eoghan asked.

"New York," Ulrik said. "We sent Dorian there to locate an ancient artifact that we believe has some connection to the Others. While he was there, he was stabbed with a black blade."

Eoghan's brows snapped together. "You can't mean the black knife. The one used by the first Fae murderer?"

"The verra one," V said.

Eoghan closed his eyes briefly.

"The man who stabbed Dorian was mortal, but he claimed to be a Druid. And Usaeil gave him the dagger," Ulrik said.

Eoghan looked down at the Tracker and shook his head. "If Usaeil can make such creatures, why would she need to join forces with Druids?"

V made a sound at the back of his throat. "Because there's been no being who could come close to competing with dragon magic. But somehow, the mix of Druid and Fae magic does it."

"A mix of good and evil," Eoghan added.

Ulrik nodded slowly. "If the magic of the Others can affect us so—"

"Then what will it do to the Fae?" Eoghan finished and lifted his gaze to the Dragon King. "It's time Death learns all of this."

V lifted a shoulder. "Get her here then."

Ulrik bowed his head in agreement.

Eoghan then said, "Death. Cael."

Within seconds, both stood before him. Erith's lavender eyes moved to the two Dragon Kings, while Cael's gaze locked on the Tracker.

"Erith," Cael murmured.

She looked down and saw the creature and took a step back. "What is this?"

"A Tracker," Eoghan explained.

Death shook her head of long, black hair. "This can't be."

"I'm afraid it is." Eoghan glanced at the two Kings who stood staring at the couple.

Cael squatted next to the Tracker and grasped its face, turning the head side to side. He then lifted the arms and rolled the beast onto its side before letting it return to its back. Cael stood and exchanged a look with Erith.

It was Death who turned to the Dragon Kings. "I would think Constantine would be here."

Ulrik's lips twisted. "He would be if he could. The problem is, Usaeil took him."

"That can't be possible," Cael stated.

V gave Cael a dry look. "I assure you, it is. Now, it's debatable whether Ubitch is holding Con or if Con is letting her think she is."

"It has to be the latter," Erith stated.

Ulrik frowned and tilted his head to her. "Why do you say that?"

Her lavender gaze met his silver one. "Because I've given Con three gifts. One allows him to move through time."

"I fucking knew it," V said beneath his breath.

Ulrik nodded slightly. "So, you think he would use it to get free."

"I think he would," Cael said. "And I don't know him like you Kings do."

Eoghan listened to everything with interest. The more he heard, the more he agreed with Erith and Cael. There was no way Usaeil, no matter how much power she claimed to have, would be able to hold Constantine.

But that brought another thought.

"You don't think Con would join her, do you?" Eoghan asked.

If looks could kill, he would've been incinerated on the spot by both Ulrik and V.

Eoghan held up his hands. "It was just a thought."

"Con wants nothing to do with her," V stated.

All anger and concern were wiped from Ulrik's visage. "Do you know what makes Con so good at being King of Dragon Kings? Because he has—and will—sacrifice his own happiness to do whatever is right for the Dragon Kings."

"Eoghan has a point, though," Cael said. "What if Con sees this as something right for the Kings?"

V shook his head harder. "Never."

"I agree with V and Ulrik," Erith said. "I've seen for myself the sacrifices Con has made for his brethren. He would never join Usaeil."

Eoghan jerked his chin to the Tracker. "We need to get this back to the other Reapers. They need to look at it to see if they can figure out if it was Light or Dark before becoming . . . this."

"Rhi needs to know of these," V said.

Ulrik blew out a breath. "So does Balladyn."

Erith nodded. "Agreed."

V glanced at Ulrik. "We'll tell Rhi."

"We can inform Balladyn, as well," Ulrik said.

Death held up a hand. "The Reapers will do that. I warned Rhi that her time was running out. It looks as if it's gone now."

"Meaning?" Ulrik asked.

Eoghan watched Erith carefully. He, as well as all the Reapers, had been trying to figure out why Death's focus had been so intent on Rhi. Maybe now he'd find out.

It was a full minute of silence before Erith said, "Because it's Rhi's destiny. But I can only give her so long before I step in and send my Reapers to claim Usaeil's soul."

"Then we need to find Rhi now," Ulrik said and touched the silver bracelet on his wrist before teleporting back to Dreagan.

She shouldn't like being at the Light Castle. And yet, Maeve did. She swallowed and let her gaze move slower this time to get a better look at things.

It had been impossible to miss all the brilliant white marble the first time she'd walked hurriedly through the castle. This time, she noticed the glittering crystal and dazzling gold that she'd overlooked before.

Maeve felt Bradach's gaze on her, but she didn't care. She didn't stop staring at the Light who milled around, going about their lives, unaware of the storm that was headed their way. She took in their easy smiles and laughter. The bright clothes that matched the array of flowers everywhere.

Plants were in vases on tables, hanging from hooks, and even draped down long columns. Their fragrance filled the air, giving the castle an otherworldly feel.

It all coalesced into a vibrant, effervescent atmosphere that made Maeve feel . . . good.

"Don't let the bright clothes and smiles fool you," Bradach whispered in her ear. "They're a bloodthirsty lot."

She turned her head toward him while keeping her gaze on the others and said in a low tone, "Not compared to the Dark."

"I can't argue with that."

Maeve met his gaze then. She couldn't remember if she'd put up her glamour before he arrived at her home. Had her eyes been red? Surely if he'd seen them in their natural state, he would've said something.

"We're here," she said. "Now what? How do you think we can hurt Usaeil?"

Bradach shot her a wink. It was so unexpected that Maeve simply stood there as he took her hand and led her into the mix of people.

It didn't seem to matter that it was night. There was a large number of Fae at the castle. Then again, there were always Dark at the palace. It must be the same for the Light. Why that surprised Maeve, she had no idea.

All these years, she had assumed there were vast differences between the Light and the Dark. Now, she saw firsthand that that wasn't the case at all. There were many similarities. Unfortunately, that gave her a small kernel of hope that she could fit in with the Light when she knew that she never would. All she knew was Dark.

No matter what appearances she might perceive, the simple fact that no Dark walked the castle was all the answer she needed. She'd been raised a Dark. There was no getting around that fact. It was better that she remain there.

Bradach suddenly stopped. Maeve found him looking at her, a deep frown on his brow.

"What is it?" he asked.

She shrugged and shook her head. "Nothing."

He stared a long moment before a muscle jumped in his jaw. "You still don't trust me."

"I wouldn't be here if I didn't."

"And yet you won't tell me what's bothering you."

She lifted one shoulder in a shrug. It wouldn't matter if Leon were the one standing beside her, she still wouldn't share the thoughts currently running through her head. "Nothing."

Bradach continued walking, but he made sure to keep his head tilted toward her so that no one else could hear him. "Right. The fact that your eyes were silver when I arrived at your place a little while ago means nothing?"

It was a good thing he had a hold of her because Maeve tripped over her own feet and would've fallen otherwise. Her head snapped to him, but he kept his gaze forward as if he hadn't just dropped a bomb on her.

Maeve was grateful that others surrounded them so she couldn't say anything. And neither could he say more for fear that someone might hear. But the simple fact was that she didn't know how to respond to Bradach. The truth would be easy, but she couldn't tell him. Could she?

She also wasn't sure how she felt about his announcement. Was she glad that he knew? It meant that she didn't have to keep hiding it from him. Then again, it meant trying to explain something that she'd kept to herself for eons.

A shiver went through her when he released her hand and wrapped an arm around her. It reminded her of how he'd pulled her into his arms after finding her kneeling over the dead Tracker.

No one had ever dared such a thing before. It felt . . . Her thoughts halted as emotions choked her. In all her long life, the only one who had ever held her had been her father. Even her lovers hadn't done such a thing. She knew she was partly responsible given how she carried herself and what she showed to others.

Bradach hadn't cared. He hadn't asked, hadn't given her time to refuse. He simply pulled her against him and gave her comfort that he'd somehow known she needed.

Maeve knew that his arm around her now was more for show than comfort, and she hated herself for liking it so much. Needing it. Damn him for giving her a taste of something she'd convinced herself that she didn't need.

Bradach lived in a world Maeve could never be a part of, and she knew that if she pursued something between them, it could only be for a short time. And she didn't want that.

Maeve wanted . . . She didn't know exactly what she wanted. But when she was with Bradach, she felt alive. Her pulse quickened when he was near, and the sound of his voice made something inside her shiver in sensuous delight.

She craved his nearness to the point that she didn't like being apart from him.

And when he showed up in her room tonight, she had been so pleased to see him that the fear that had taken her while she fought the Tracker had vanished the moment her gaze landed on him.

These were thoughts she would never dare tell a soul—not even Leon. Emotions choked her when she thought of her dear friend. She would find him. Her thoughts about Bradach were private thoughts, dreams really. Because no one was more aware of her reality than she.

Maeve knew how important it was to be conscious of her surroundings and alert to anyone and anything, and yet she'd let her mind wander. Why? Because she was with Bradach. Because she trusted him. Completely.

That right there should make her run far and fast because the only one she'd ever trusted was Leon. Instead, she shifted slightly closer to Bradach as if her body knew what her mind couldn't quite grasp yet.

His fingers curled around her waist. She liked to think it was a possessive move, but she knew it was only in her mind. But she was going to enjoy this for however long it lasted. She blinked, realizing that Bradach had taken them away from the others down a long corridor.

The walls were painted with scenes from the Fae Wars. To her surprise, she saw a dragon. It was difficult to miss since it was gold and flying above Usaeil, who stood on the ground with the army behind her.

Maeve halted, unable to look away. All Fae, whether alive during the Fae Wars or not, knew how the Dragon Kings had fought against the Dark. Then the Light had joined the Kings. Some said it was the Light who swung the tide of the war, but Maeve knew that was a load of shite. The truth was, the Kings would've won anyway. The Light joining them just allowed them to do it quicker.

"That's Constantine," Bradach said.

His arm was still around her. She could feel his warmth seep into her. And she had the insane urge to lean her head slightly to the side and rest it against him. He wouldn't pull away. She knew that. But she still didn't give in to the impulse.

"Have you ever met a Dragon King?" she asked, looking at him.

Bradach glanced her way before his gaze returned to the painting. "I have."

"Really?" She was surprised by his admission. Then again, everything about Bradach amazed her.

He grinned slightly. "You sound impressed."

"I am."

"Want to meet one?"

She blinked, suddenly unsure if he was teasing her or not. "I'm a Dark."

"Are you?" he asked, a black brow quirked.

Maeve turned her head away, no longer wanting to talk. She wished she'd never stopped to take a closer look at the mural.

"The Kings don't care," Bradach said.

Then, without another word, he turned them and continued on. Maeve was grateful that he'd ended the conversation. At least she was until they walked through a set of doors, and she realized that they were in someone's chambers.

"Easy."

She shot Bradach a dark look as she pulled out of his arms and backed up toward the door. "Don't tell me that. Where are we?"

"I'm looking for Inen."

"Who?" she asked with a frown.

"He's Captain of the Queen's Guard."

Maeve took another step back, suddenly wary. "Why would you want him?"

Bradach sighed. "I really wish you'd trust me."

"Perhaps if you told me what you were doing."

"Inen is friends with someone I know."

Maeve narrowed her eyes and crossed her arms over her chest. "Who?"

"Rhi."

Shock reverberated through her. "Rhi? As in the infamous Rhiannon?"

"The very one," Bradach said nonchalantly.

"You know Rhi?"

He shrugged. "Rhi and Inen are friends. I want to find him because there's a chance Usaeil has killed him."

"How could she do that? Others would notice."

"She's used glamour to masquerade as him."

Maeve widened her eyes. "How do you know this?"

"A Dragon King told me."

Just what had she stepped into? She licked her lips and glanced behind her before she shut the door and walked to him. "Who are you really?"

"Someone who's on your side."

"I doubt that."

His silver eyes sparkled with a hint of anger. "I don't lie."

She'd made him angry. Good. She wanted to see how far she could push him. Maeve let her lips curve into a smile. "Ever?"

"Ever."

"So, I can ask you anything?"

He tightened his jaw. "I won't lie, but that doesn't mean I can tell you everything."

"Understood," she said and turned away, intending to take a look around the room while thinking of how else she could push his buttons.

"Perhaps we can share secrets."

She stilled. Maeve should've seen that coming. But she hadn't. That's what Bradach did to her. He set her on her heels, turned her world upside down. He shook things up.

In all, he made life exciting again.

She wasn't sure how to answer, or even if she wanted to. To give someone her secret gave them power over her. That wasn't something she could dare.

Then his voice reached her like a seductive caress. "Afraid of trusting me?"

Maeve slowly turned to face him. "You would trust me?"

"Does it matter what I answer? Because we both know you won't tell me anything."

He pivoted away and began searching the chamber. Maeve didn't move, not even when Bradach called Inen's name. She was irrationally angry at his statement. Not because it was true, but because she wanted to tell him her secret.

"There's nothing here," Bradach said after several moments. "And if Inen is alive, he'd have come when I called. Especially when he realized I was in his chamber."

Maeve nodded, unable to come up with a suitable reply. They walked out of the room and back into the corridor in silence. Bradach's arm wasn't around her now, and he kept at least a foot between them at all times.

It was for the best. Maeve knew it, even as it irritated her. No matter her attraction to Bradach, the notion of them together would only bring heartache. And she didn't need that in her life.

However, if she'd thought they were leaving the castle, she was sorely mistaken. Bradach led her through a maze of hallways and up three flights of stairs before he walked through another doorway.

Maeve followed, only to realize that they were in another set of chambers. These were well appointed with all the riches a Fae could expect at the castle.

"Whose room are we in now?" Maeve asked after Bradach had lowered himself into a chair covered in a rich blue velvet.

His silver gaze lifted and locked with hers. "Ours."

CHAPTER
sixteen

The subtle shift in her expression was hard to miss. Then again, Bradach had been looking for it. He could've made sure they had two rooms, but that wasn't what he wanted.

No matter how much he might try to deny the passion that raged like a violent storm unleashed, he couldn't ignore it any longer.

Every second beside Maeve tempted him . . . enticed him . . . was the most beautiful, delicious kind of torment. Bradach didn't know when he'd decided to pursue her. It was probably the moment he'd found her standing over the Tracker. All he knew was that the caution in his brain flipped off.

And all he wanted was her.

To hold her.

Seduce her.

Kiss her.

Make love to her.

She hadn't uttered a word since he told her the room was theirs. He half expected her to balk and demand one of her own. The fact that she didn't made him inwardly smile.

He was under no illusions that he'd won her over. But he'd taken a huge step—one that she had allowed. He'd realized quickly that she was up for any challenge. Even one that included a stay at the Light Castle.

Maeve tucked her hair behind one ear and turned her back to him in order to look over the room. He wasn't fooled. She was getting her bearings. Not that he minded. He'd had to do that several times when she was near. That's how she upended his carefully thought out existence.

"You don't seem at all concerned about Usaeil finding us," she said as she walked to a large vase full of bright pink and blue flowers.

Bradach watched as she leaned her hand on the table, bringing her face within inches of the blooms. He waited for her to inhale. As she did, her eyes closed briefly.

His balls tightened watching her. She was stunning. And her raspy voice made his blood heat every time she spoke. It was a good thing she had no idea that she caused such havoc, or she might use it against him.

Her head suddenly turned so their gazes clashed. She raised a brow, waiting for him to answer.

"I'm not worried," he finally replied. "Usaeil is otherwise occupied for the moment. She won't return here anytime soon because she believes no one would dare come to the castle."

Maeve shifted so that one hip rested against the table. "Why are we here exactly?"

"Usaeil's absence gives us an opportunity."

"To do what?" Maeve said with a confused shake of her head. "She has ruled the Light longer than any Fae before her."

Bradach pushed to his feet and walked to stand before Maeve. "If Usaeil spent as much time with her people as she did in front of a movie camera, then I might say you had a point. But she's let the Light flounder for centuries. There is dissent among them."

"Is there? Because I didn't see any."

He merely smiled. "It's not what people are saying. It's what they aren't saying. You run a business. It's much like ruling. How do you think your company would do if you no longer saw to the day-to-day?"

She swallowed and lifted one shoulder. "It would be all right for a little while. Leon would see to that. But you're right. Anything longer than a few months would call attention to the company and me. My enemies would come in droves."

"They wouldn't band together and attack you," he said. "They'd come at you one at a time."

She nodded slowly. "To discover my weak spots. Once they found one, they'd ruthlessly strike."

"That's no different than what occurs in a monarchy. Do you think Balladyn alerted Taraeth that he was about to remove him as king and take the throne?"

Maeve's head tilted to the side as her eyes narrowed slightly. "Every time you say Balladyn's name, I have the sense that you don't really care for him. And yet I got the feeling that he genuinely respects you."

Bradach looked away. He'd thought he'd masked his irritation well. It seemed he needed to work on that. "What would you think if I told you that I haven't known Balladyn long. That I used him to get close to you?"

"I'd say it was a smart and very bold move. One I'd have taken."

His head snapped to her. He'd thought she might be outraged, but there wasn't a shred of anger in her voice or countenance.

"You might not have known him long, but he knew you. Right?" Maeve asked.

Bradach nodded his head.

Maeve shifted slightly, bringing her closer to him. Bradach reached up and smoothed away a strand of hair that had gotten caught in her eyelashes. Then he let his fingertips slowly caress down the side of her face.

He gazed into her pale silver orbs. Bradach couldn't remember ever yearning for a woman's touch as he did with Maeve.

Everything ceased and disappeared but her. Bradach lowered his head, giving Maeve ample time to move away. Blood rushed straight to his cock when she lifted her face to his. He wrapped one arm around her as the other rested on her hip. A groan filled him when her hands landed on his chest.

Their lips met, softly, hesitantly. He held still a moment before he kissed her again and again.

And again.

"This is wrong," she whispered as she pulled back slightly.

He tightened his arms, praying she didn't pull away. "Nothing that feels this good can be wrong."

"You aren't Dark."

"Neither are you."

Sadness filled her eyes. "I am."

He couldn't come up with an argument to make her stay. He could feel her pulling away, and it was like a blade right through his gut.

"Do you want me?" he asked.

She blinked up at him, a small frown on her brow. "Yes."

"And I want you. Fek everything else. Why should any of it matter if we want each other?"

Maeve's lips curved into a grin. "That's fine for now. But what about after?"

"I'm not thinking about that."

"One of us should." She sighed and lowered her head.

Bradach was losing her before he'd ever even had her. He had one more chance to change her mind. "Maeve, when was the last time you felt this?"

There was a pause of silence before she looked up at him. "I don't think I ever have."

"Neither have I. Fate put us together. I don't want to waste such an opportunity thinking of tomorrow." He slid his palm around the nape of her neck, feeling the cool strands of her hair on the back of his hand.

"I don't want you to regret this later. You look at me now and see a Light."

He was shaking his head before she finished. "What I see is a woman who sets my blood on fire. I see a woman who I hunger for like no other."

Desire sparked in her eyes before she grasped the back of his head and rose up on her tiptoes to place her lips against his. It was all the invitation he needed.

Bradach wound his arms around her and held her tight as he slipped his tongue past her lips to duel with hers. He deepened the kiss, needing to be closer to her.

The taste of her was sublime.

The feel of her was incredible.

But he needed more. He needed inside her, to feel her hot body surrounding him.

Just as he was thinking of removing her clothes, they disappeared. Along with his. Bradach paused long enough to look down at her.

Maeve grinned and shrugged. "Why waste time taking off clothes when we have magic?"

"I like the way you think."

"Then you'll really like what I'm thinking about now," she stated with a seductive look.

Bradach lifted his gaze over her head to the bed behind her. He bent slightly and tightened his arms before he straightened, lifting her. Maeve laughed. The sound was so beautiful and so surprising that, for a moment, he couldn't move.

He stared at the bright smile and the joy mixed with desire in her eyes, and Bradach suddenly wanted to see that expression on her face every day.

When she wrapped her legs around his waist, it pulled him out of his thoughts. Somehow, he got his legs to work again and made his way to the bed. He stopped beside it. There were things he needed to say, but he wasn't sure how. Or even if he should.

They lodged in his chest, refusing to move. They mixed with emotions he couldn't begin to describe and caused a storm within him. Then Maeve rested a hand over his heart and leaned forward to place her lips on his. She broke through whatever had held him.

He placed a knee on the bed and bent forward, holding her against him until he lowered her to the bed. Only then did he release her, and just so he could run his hands all over her amazing body.

"Beautiful," he murmured as he leisurely kissed her.

She sighed while her hands moved over his back. "You haven't even seen me."

He lifted his head to look down at her. "I don't have to see you with my eyes to know you're gorgeous. My hands are learning you. The silky texture of your skin, the softness of your curves."

Bradach held her gaze as his hand ran up her thigh. "I feel the firmness of your muscles." He groaned, grinning. "The flare of your hips is perfect."

"Perfect?" she asked with a grin.

"Mm-hmm. Curvy, just as I like it." He let his hand continue upward. "The indent of your waist is incredibly sexy. Then there are your breasts."

She gasped as he cupped one and let his fingers flick lightly over a nipple.

Bradach didn't hold back his smile at her reaction. "Full and pert. A precise fill for my hand."

The way her chest heaved, and her pulse turned erratic at the base of her throat made his blood pound faster.

"All woman," he murmured before kissing her neck up to her ear. "And utterly stunning."

Her moan when he suckled on her ear lobe was just what he needed to hear. He massaged her breast before he rolled her nipple between his fingers, all while sliding a leg between hers.

She rocked her hips against him, her nails digging into his back. He kissed down her neck until he wrapped his lips around her nipple. Heat ran through him when she arched her back and tightened her legs around him.

Just as he moved his hand toward her sex, Maeve tossed him onto his back and straddled him. He smiled up at her, his stomach doing a little flip-flop when her silver eyes met his. She was the epitome of sensuality—without even trying.

It was as natural to her as breathing. And she had no idea of her allure. Or perhaps she did. He didn't know or care. All that mattered was that she was in his arms.

She sat up and leaned her head to the side. Her wealth of midnight hair fell over one shoulder as she smoothed her hands over his chest.

"It's my turn," she said with a sexy smile.

Bradach's hands ran up her legs to her hips. "I'm all yours, sweetheart."

Slowly, she leaned over him until her breasts rubbed against his chest. Her lips hovered over his. When he tried to kiss her, she pulled back, a teasing glint in her eyes.

"You don't show off your body. You keep it hidden, your clothes like your armor. But what a body," Maeve said and closed her eyes.

She sat up again and smoothed her hands over his shoulders, down his arms and back up again before moving to his stomach. "Sinew as hard as granite. Every muscle honed and sculpted. A warrior." Her eyes opened to meet his. "Who wants to hide that fact?"

Before he could reply, she reached behind her and grasped his arousal. Her hand moved up and down his length. He shifted his hips in time with her movements.

In short order, she had him so worked up that if he didn't watch it, he'd orgasm. That's when he realized what she was doing. Teasing him as he had her.

"I like having you under my spell," she said in a sexy whisper.

In the next heartbeat, he had her on her back again. "I was yours from the first moment I saw you."

CHAPTER

seventeen

The flutter in Maeve's stomach at Bradach's statement was the only warning she got that things had progressed much farther than she'd realized.

She couldn't look away from his silver eyes. In one instant, she realized that she was the one utterly ensnared. It didn't matter how or when—only that it had happened. And she wasn't prepared for it.

If she were smart, she'd stop this insanity right now and leave. She'd forget all about Bradach and the incredible way he made her feel. She'd ignore the pounding of her heart when he was near and how she craved the taste of his lips.

And she would turn her back on anything to do with bringing Usaeil down.

Because giving in to the hunger, the longing to be with Bradach was leading her down a path she didn't know how to walk. One that could well end in the very reckoning she'd avoided her entire life.

Every decision she'd made, every step she'd taken from the moment she grabbed the reins of her father's business created an environment of her making. It was all now in jeopardy. She knew it. Accepted it.

Despite comprehending it, she remained in Bradach's arms, gazing up into his face. In that instant, a defining moment, she decided to do the unthinkable and be rash. She grabbed hold of the unknown, grasped a frightening future that could well be the end of her.

All for however long she could spend sharing her body with Bradach.

She didn't care about his secrets. She didn't worry that he had all but guessed hers. She didn't care about anything other than the hunger for him that thrummed within her, growing with every heartbeat.

Maeve reached up and cupped Bradach's cheek. The rush of feelings within her remained. She might be taking a step in a different direction, but she wasn't foolish enough to try and put into words whatever it was that was swirling within her now.

It was then that she realized how long she had been staring into his eyes, lost in thought. He hadn't pushed her to share what she was thinking. But now she wanted to know what was going through his mind.

"There's still time for you to say no."

Maeve blinked at his statement. Then she smiled. "The time for me to say that passed the moment I agreed to help you locate Usaeil. I knew what I was getting into."

He quirked a black brow, a crooked grin on his lips. "Did you?"

"Well, not precisely," she admitted with a chuckle. "But I wanted to see where this would all lead."

"This could end in disaster."

She shrugged and let her hand run down his neck to his chest. "For the first time, I'm doing something that feels right. I always win. So, if this time I lose, I'll have done it by doing something good."

His silver eyes narrowed. "No harm will come to you."

"You can't promise that."

"I can. I just did. And there's nothing you can do about it."

Maeve couldn't help but smile. That's what Bradach did to her. He made it feel as though everything would be fine, that she was safe. No one—not even her father—had ever made her feel such a way.

"Shut up and kiss me," she told Bradach.

He laughed softly and lowered his head until their lips met. She sighed as his tongue met hers. The kiss began slow, languid, but within moments, they were clinging to each other as a fire raged between them—through them.

She surrendered completely. There was no other way with Bradach. And as she gave herself to him, the niggle of worry in the back of her mind ceased. As if she had done the one thing that righted everything once more.

Maeve rocked her hips against Bradach as his arousal pressed against her. It wasn't enough. She needed more. She needed him. Now.

"I can't wait," she said between kisses.

Bradach shifted, and the next moment, she felt the head of his cock rub against her sex. She sucked in a breath at the amazing sensation. Then, he was inside her.

She sank her nails into his back, her eyes closing at the exquisite feeling of him filling her, stretching her. He entered her slowly, inch by inch until he was fully seated. Only then did she open her eyes to find him staring down at her.

"This is where I've wanted to be for a while," he confessed.

She swallowed, her stomach quivering at his admission. And it gave her the courage to voice her own declaration. "This is where I want you to stay."

"That's good because I have no plans to leave."

Whatever words Maeve formed in her head vanished when he began to move. His length slid in and out of her, taking her higher and higher each time. It felt incredible, as if her body had been waiting for his all this time.

It frightened her a little, but it was too amazing for the fear to take a firm hold.

In the next moment, Bradach rolled them so he was on his back. Maeve smiled down at him as she found herself straddling him.

By the stars! Maeve had a hold on him that Bradach had never experienced before. He knew that whatever was occurring between them was special.

It also scared the holy fek out of him.

But he couldn't seem to stop—or even slow—whatever was happening.

He placed his hands on Maeve's hips as she straightened and shook out her hair. The long length fell around her like an inky curtain. The moment she rocked her hips, he groaned. The pleasure was intense and, oh, so wonderful.

Bradach grasped her breasts and teased her nipples, which caused her to moan. She dropped her head back so the ends of her hair teased his thighs.

His hands caressed lower to hold onto her sides. Every movement she made caused her breasts to sway, which only made him crave her more. Everything she did was sensual and utterly sexy. She had him wrapped so firmly around her finger that he was ready and willing to do whatever she wanted.

When she ran her hands over her breasts while moaning, he had to grip her hips to keep her still lest he spill his seed right then.

"Woman," he said roughly.

Her head lifted, and she locked her gaze with his. "I'm so close."

He slid his hand down her stomach until his thumb found her swollen nub. Bradach slowly rubbed her clit, which caused her hips to buck. The faster he stroked, the quicker she rode him.

Then she gasped, her hands falling on his chest as she leaned forward. Her body tightened as she let out a pleasure-filled cry.

That's all it took to send Bradach barreling toward his own climax. As he held her hips and thrust upward, he felt her body clenching around him. The ecstasy was unlike anything he'd experienced before.

It wrapped around them like a cocoon, swaddling them in bliss and shutting out the outside world. When she had milked the last from him, Maeve slumped forward. He wrapped his arms around her and held her tightly, his cheek pressed against the top of her head.

He closed his eyes as contentment settled around him. Bradach searched his mind for the last time he'd felt such peace, and to his surprise, he couldn't remember a single instance.

And yet he'd found it in the arms of a Dark.

He didn't know how long they lay together before he realized that their breaths matched. There was so much he needed to be doing, but he didn't want to shatter the serenity they'd found.

"Please tell me we get to do that again," Maeve asked.

He smiled and kissed her temple. "As many times as you want."

"Then you might as well get comfortable because I don't think I want to leave this bed."

"Mmm. That sounds like a perfect plan." He ran his hands up and down her back before squeezing her.

After a few minutes, she said, "But we can't stay, can we?"

"No."

Maeve rolled off him onto her side to face him. She said nothing, simply looked at him. All kinds of words ran through Bradach's head, but none of them seemed the right thing to say. He couldn't find the appropriate words. They needed to be perfect —and yet, there was nothing.

"I understand," Maeve said with a smile.

But there was a sadness in it that hadn't been there before. Bradach didn't like it. He wanted it gone. Forever.

"Think of it as paused. You'll not get rid of me that easily," he told her as he faced her on his side. And because he couldn't stand not touching her, he rested a hand on her hip.

She glanced down and licked her lips. "You're looking for your friend, and we're no closer to finding him. Usaeil knows I've helped you since she sent the Tracker after me. I'm guessing that everyone who worked for me is now dead. The waters are muddied to such an extent now that I don't know how we can hurt her."

"There are ways. For one, she needs to have others adore her. Remember the discontent in her court that I told you about?"

Maeve nodded.

"We're going to use it."

A frown deepened her brow. "You trust those Fae?"

"There comes a time when you have to have faith that things will work out. Will we be betrayed? Without a doubt. But we have to be smart about who we use and who we tell."

"Tell?" she asked curiously.

Bradach ran his thumb in a circle on her hip. "I think it's time some of Usaeil's secrets come out."

The worried look returned to Maeve's face. "You're playing with fire."

"Do you have a better idea?"

"No," she said with a shake of her head. "Your plan hinges on others doing what you expect them to."

"That's because we're going to make sure they do. And you're an expert in that department."

Her eyes widened as she chuckled softly. "Me?"

"Absolutely."

"You've never seen me do anything like that."

He shrugged. "Maybe not, but if the King of the Dark is impressed by you, then you must be very good at what you do."

Maeve gazed at him for a heartbeat. "Now Balladyn's word means something?"

Bradach was taken aback by her observation. Especially since he hadn't realized just how much stock he'd put in Balladyn's praise of Maeve until he told her.

He shrugged. "Apparently so."

"It's obvious you . . . dislike . . . the Dark. I gather one hurt you? You're a Light, aren't you?"

Bradach rolled onto his back. He hadn't expected her to ask such a question, but he should have. He hadn't bothered to hide his aversion to Balladyn well enough earlier. That was a mistake he usually never made.

Either he was slipping, or Maeve read people really well. He liked to think that she had been able to read him rather than him failing to mask his true feelings.

"You don't have to tell me," she said.

He turned his head to her then rolled back to face her. "It's not that. It's just not something I speak about often."

"I shouldn't have asked."

The moment she began to roll away, he reached out and grasped her arm to stop her. "You're right. I'm Light. I just needed a moment to gather myself. I can talk about it."

At least, he hoped he could.

CHAPTER

eighteen

Where to start? Bradach had never retold the story. He'd replayed it so many times in his head that it felt as if he had told everyone in the world. Now, he really hoped he could get the words out to tell Maeve.

"I was a middle child," he began. "I had an older brother and a younger sister. Brian was the epitome of the firstborn son. Everything he did, everything he touched was golden. There wasn't a thing he couldn't do or a woman he couldn't get. I idolized him. I wanted to hate him for being so perfect, but I couldn't. He was a good guy. The kind that would give you the shirt off his back if you needed it."

Maeve grinned. "He sounds nice."

"Intelligent, strong, honorable, and kind. Everyone loved Brian. The same with my little sister. Bree was the sweetest soul you would ever find. She spent her days with animals. If there was a wounded one, then it would find its way to her so she could heal it."

Bradach grinned as he thought of the badger Bree had once found in a snare and brought home. His parents had freaked out. But not Brian. No, his older brother had helped Bree create a nest for it.

"How was it being a middle child?" Maeve asked. "I was an only child, so I have no experience in any of this."

He shrugged. "We were two years apart, and we did bicker occasionally. But, oddly enough, we got along for the most part. Brian knew exactly what he wanted to do with his life. He wanted to join the Light army, and because I followed him in everything, I decided that's what I would do, as well."

Maeve put her hand atop his. "Did something happen in battle?"

"We were in several, but we survived every one. I'm still not sure how that happened exactly. Several of the skirmishes I was in were severe."

"Proof of how good you are."

He lifted one shoulder in a shrug. "My parents were relieved when we returned home. During the time we were gone, my sister had made her own way in the world. She'd met a man who Brian and I instantly disliked. We soon learned that our parents weren't thrilled with him either."

"Did you try to talk to Bree about it?" Maeve asked.

Bradach nodded. "To disastrous ends. When Bree learned that none of us liked him, she ran off with him. It broke my mother's heart and tore my father up in ways that made me realize how much we all meant to him. I was so angry at Bree for running off that I was about ready to forget her."

Maeve gasped in outrage, her eyes wide. "You can't be serious?"

"I was at the time. When I cooled off, I would've felt differently. Brian didn't give me time to get there. He said he was going after her, so of course, I went with him. We told my parents what we were doing. My father wanted to come, but we convinced him to remain behind. It took less than a week to locate Bree and the man she was with."

Bradach stopped as memories of the hovel he'd found his sister in bombarded him. Maeve scooted closer to him. She didn't say anything, just put her arms around him and held him.

It was several minutes later before he could continue. "Our instincts about my sister's lover were right. He wasn't just weak, he was a coward. When they ran out of money and places to go, he sold her."

Maeve's arms tightened around Bradach because she knew where this tragic story was headed.

"He sold her to a group of Dark, who raped her repeatedly. There was nothing but a shell left of her by the time we found her."

Maeve's eyes misted at the pain she heard in Bradach's voice. She swallowed and tried to hold in her tears.

"Brian went berserk when he saw Bree's man sitting not far from her, observing it all," Bradach continued. "Brian tore him to shreds. And I didn't stop my brother. I watched him doing the very thing I wanted to do. I battled the Dark to keep them away from him, and by the time I finished, I turned to find Brian sitting on the floor, holding Bree in his arms. I took a step toward them when Brian broke her neck. It was a blessing, I know. There was nothing but a body left of my sister. And when Brian looked up at me, his eyes were red."

Maeve's heart broke for Bradach. "I'm so sorry."

"I should've killed my brother right then, but I didn't. I had already lost Bree. I couldn't bear to have Brian's death on my conscience, as well. But I should've done it."

"You were thinking of your parents," she said.

He shook his head. "I told my parents that Brian died in battle. But that's not why I should've killed him."

"Then why?" Maeve asked after a brief pause.

Bradach lifted his head to look at her. "Because he betrayed me and then murdered me."

Maeve's mind locked on the word betrayal, so it took her a moment to realize that he had said something else. She frowned at him in confusion. "What do you mean he murdered you? You're very much alive."

Bradach rolled onto his back and put an arm under his head. "The people who claim that blood is thicker than water don't know what they're saying. Family means nothing when one turns Dark."

"He lost his way," Maeve argued.

"Brian embraced the darkness within him. He loved being Dark, and he used it against me."

Maeve wanted to reach for Bradach, to give him comfort, but she wasn't sure she was doing it correctly. Or maybe he just didn't want it.

They lay in silence for several minutes as she thought over everything he'd told her. She guessed there was still much more to Bradach, but it was obvious by the way his voice sometimes broke as he spoke that he couldn't say it all.

She wanted to pretend that she didn't have a story to share, but there was no denying it. If he could relive such a heartrending tale, then she could tell hers.

"My father was a ruthless man. At least he was to everyone except me. I lived in a sheltered world during my early years. I knew only happiness and love. Until I realized that everyone had red eyes except for me. When I asked my father about it, that's when he told me about the Light and Dark Fae. At first, I didn't understand the difference because my father doted on me so. In order to show me, he let me listen in on one of his meetings. That's when I saw the other side to him."

"And your mother?" Bradach asked.

She shrugged. "She died hours after I was born. My father rarely spoke of her. It was just the two of us. And Leon. Leon was the son of my father's friend. Leon was the only friend I had for years and years. We were inseparable. As I began to learn about the business and all the different dealings my father had, Leon remained beside me like a bodyguard. Soon, he became the only other person I trusted besides my father."

Bradach turned his head to Maeve. "No one noticed your silver eyes?"

"I used glamour. My father thought it would be best, and we agreed that I would never tell anyone. I mastered the glamour so well that it became second nature. Despite the lie, life was good. I fully realized the man my father was, but he was someone different with me. To me, that was his true self. The rest was just an act. But my world upended when he was murdered."

A frown marred Bradach's brow. "Someone killed him? Did you find out who?"

"No, and I've never stopped looking. It happened in his office, which limited the number of people who could've done it. Yet that didn't offer up anyone. I had a choice to make. And quickly. Did I take over in my father's place, or did I step aside, knowing that one of his enemies would likely swoop in to claim the business—and kill me in the process. I had no interest in dying, nor did I want to spend my life hiding, so I did the only thing I could."

"You took over," Bradach said.

She licked her lips and sighed. "The first century was the most trying. Every time I turned around, someone was trying to deceive me. I lost count of the number of times someone tried to kill me. And through it all, Leon remained by my side. I took a page from my father's book and developed a persona that I kept in place anytime I left my room. I gave no quarter and never exhibited mercy of any kind. Finally, others began to realize I had what it took to run the business."

"And the silver in your hair without the red eyes?"

She smiled since she'd known he was going to ask. "Throughout the years, I've had to order some deaths. While I didn't carry them out myself, I did make the decree. With each one, my hair became more silver."

"But because you've not killed anyone, your eyes haven't turned red."

"Now you know my secret."

In a blink, he was leaning over her. "That's nothing to be ashamed of."

"It is to the Dark."

"But you aren't Dark."

"I'm not Light either. I don't fit in either world."

He bent and pressed his lips against hers for a heartbeat. "You belong in mine."

"Do I? You despise the Dark. Which means me."

"Like you said, you aren't Dark," he replied with a grin. "And how do you feel about the Light?"

"I hold no ill will toward them."

His smile widened. "Good."

Maeve wound her arms around Bradach's neck. She didn't even second-guess her trust in him. Somehow, she knew that Bradach wouldn't share her secret.

He leaned his forehead against hers and let out a long breath. Maeve wanted to stop time, but she knew their interlude was over. There was too much at stake for them to remain in the room together.

"Our time has ended," she said.

Bradach lifted his head. "For the moment. I will have you back in a bed as soon as I can. I'm not nearly done with you."

That sent a shiver of excitement through her. She wanted to ask Bradach if that was a promise, but she knew better than most that such assurances couldn't be made.

She smiled when he continued staring at her. When she tried to get up, he refused to let her.

"You want it, too, right?" Bradach asked.

Maeve met his silver gaze. "Of course."

"I'm getting the feeling that's not the case."

"I do want you and to be back in a bed with you again, but I'm a realist."

He frowned, his lips twisting. "What's that supposed to mean?"

"It means that anything can happen. It means that Usaeil will figure out soon enough that her Tracker didn't kill me, and she'll send another."

Bradach shrugged. "You'll kill it as you did the first."

"She'll keep sending them."

"Then I'll remain beside you to make sure none get to you."

Maeve sat up and pushed him so he had no choice but to sit back, as well. "I appreciate the sentiment, but I'm guessing that won't exactly fly with the people you're working with."

"No," he said with a shake of his head. Then he paused and looked away.

She touched his leg. "I've survived this long. I'll continue to do so until my time comes."

His gaze swung back to her. "I got you into this."

"That's not entirely true. You asked for my help, and I gave it. After I killed the Tracker, I could've run. But I'm here with you. That should tell you that I made this decision all on my own."

"It's not fair."

She laughed. "I said that once to my father. He told me there isn't much about life that is fair."

"I didn't tell you my secret," he said.

Maeve covered his mouth with her hand and shook her head. "I don't want to know. It's a secret because it's important."

He removed her hand. "But you told me yours."

"I told you something that you saw yourself when I didn't use glamour. I've known from the beginning that the secret you carry is a deep one. You don't share it because it's better if I don't know. So, keep it that way."

"I want you to know."

She moved onto her hands and knees and kissed him. "And that's enough for me."

nineteen

He was in over his head. Bradach knew it and didn't know how to fix the problem. Or if he even wanted to.

How had he gone from being so cool-headed and in control to feeling as if he were in the midst of ever-changing chaos as well as courting recklessness like an old friend?

Because he was being rash and careless.

Yet when Maeve was in his arms, he had to keep reminding himself that there were other duties, other people he had to take care of. His mission to find Xaneth was still paramount. In order to do that—and also have a chance at locating Constantine—he had to stop Usaeil.

If only he could just attack the queen, then this would be over.

Actually, the easiest solution was for Death to pass judgment on Usaeil and send the Reapers to collect her soul. That would solve everyone's problems. Why then were they waiting on Rhi? What was so fekking important about the Light Fae that everyone else's life was in danger?

Bradach glanced at Maeve, who walked beside him. He could ask himself that question every minute of every hour and still not get an answer. It wasn't as if he could ask Erith. Whatever Death saw in Rhi, she was keeping it to herself.

"You look concerned," Maeve said.

Bradach twisted his lips and waved away her words. "Just thinking."

"Worried."

He put his hand on her back and maneuvered her into a doorway, blocking anyone from seeing her if they happened to pass by. "We can work this two ways. Together."

"Or?" she asked when he didn't immediately continue.

"We don't interact at all. You go one way, I go the other." He didn't like that option because he wouldn't be there to protect her if anything happened.

She lifted one shoulder as she met his gaze. "We'll cover more ground that way. I vote for the second option."

"Don't let the Light fool you. This is still court."

Maeve flashed him a smile. "Don't worry about me. I've got this covered."

She rose up on her tiptoes and gave him a quick kiss before she ducked beneath his arm and walked away. Bradach turned to watch her. He wanted to call her back or go after her. It took all of his control to remain where he was and let her go.

Bradach was so focused on Maeve and his silent promise to hunt down anyone who dared to hurt her that he didn't notice that he was no longer alone.

"This has taken a turn I hadn't expected."

He froze at the sound of Eoghan's voice. Bradach then slowly pivoted to face his leader. "She's putting her life at risk to help us."

"She has no choice since Usaeil sent the Tracker after her."

Bradach slid his gaze to Maeve for one more look before she turned the corner. "And the Tracker came because Maeve told me about the place in California."

Eoghan sliced his hand through the air, his quicksilver eyes going hard. "I know better than anyone how it feels to have the one you love mixed up in our war. Maeve isn't a Halfling. She's a powerful Fae. She is also able to take care of herself, evidenced by the fact that she killed the Tracker. You need to get your head on straight."

"It is." Bradach was offended that Eoghan would suggest otherwise.

"I beg to differ."

Bradach blew out a breath and shifted away as he tried to find the calm that was usually so easy to wield. "I'm not sure what's happening to me."

"That's easy. You're falling for her."

"I don't want to."

"Love doesn't care about rules or timing, Bradach. It has its own course, and right now, it's chosen you."

He met Eoghan's gaze. "All I want to do is take her somewhere safe."

"That's the thing, my friend. There is nowhere she'll be safe as long as there are Trackers after her, and as long as the queen is alive."

"Then send Rhi after Usaeil!"

Bradach regretted the outburst as soon as it happened. He never let himself get riled, but when it came to Maeve, everything was upended.

Eoghan crossed his arms over his chest and studied Bradach for a long, silent minute. "I've no doubt that had Usaeil not taken Con, we'd be in the midst of war right this moment.

Unfortunately, her actions have thrown things out of whack. She's one against not just the Dragon Kings, not just Balladyn and the Dark Army, but also us. She doesn't stand a chance."

That's when it came to Bradach. He squeezed his eyes closed before he lifted his lids to look at Eoghan. "That's where we've messed up. She's not alone."

"A few Trackers?" Eoghan said with a shrug.

"When I went back to Maeve's and found her standing over the Tracker, we discovered everyone else gone. Everyone, Eoghan. There wasn't a single other soul on the vast estate."

Eoghan's chest expanded as he took a deep breath and slowly released it. As he did, he dropped his arms to his sides. "Fek me. Usaeil is taking them."

"Just as Bran kidnapped Dark to make his army. Usaeil is doing exactly as he did."

"Cael, Erith, and the rest of the Reapers are dissecting the Tracker, but we need one alive to really study it."

Bradach ran a hand over the back of his neck. "You may get it. Usaeil won't be happy until Maeve is dead, which means, she'll send another Tracker."

"I'll send the others to keep a lookout throughout the castle. You made a good move coming here. Usaeil won't expect that."

Bradach nodded. "I thought we were finished with this shite. First Bran, now Usaeil."

"There will always be someone like that causing trouble. For the most part, it doesn't pertain to us, but in these cases, it does."

Bradach blew out a breath. "Is there anything you can tell me about the Tracker from Maeve's?"

"He was a Light. Cael discovered who he was."

"Cael's new powers are still manifesting, huh?"

"I'm not complaining." Eoghan's smile was quick. "Keep

following your instincts. Both yours and Maeve's. We'll watch your backs."

With that, Eoghan disappeared.

Bradach walked down the quiet hallway. As he got closer to the main area of the castle, the din of conversation reached him. It became louder and louder until he stood on the fringes of it.

His gaze moved around the area, searching for any sign of Maeve. He hated when he couldn't find her, but he knew she was near. It never entered his mind that Maeve would leave. Despite her being Dark—or raised as a Dark—he knew she was honorable.

Something he'd never expected to say about a Dark.

Bradach inwardly shook himself and made his way through the throng of Fae who stood in groups. As he passed them, he listened to their conversations until he found the one he was searching for.

He purposefully bumped into an older Fae. "Pardon me. It's been a while since I've been to court. There seems to be an unusually large crowd."

The gentleman shrugged and glanced at his comrades—one woman and two men. "More and more are coming. There's . . . unrest in the Light."

"Comgall," the woman admonished while glancing warily at Bradach.

Bradach's gaze moved to her. She wasn't nearly as aged as the men, but she wasn't a youngster either. Her black hair was cut short and parted on the side. She wore no jewels to match her outfit of various shades of pink from pale to dark.

"That's the reason I'm here," Bradach said to Comgall before nodding to the other three. "Something is going on, and I want to know what it is."

Comgall shifted to make room for him. "And you are?"

"Apologies. My name is Bradach. I must admit, I've stayed away from court. Duties at home."

"Of course, of course." Comgall then motioned to the others. "This is Derry, Felim, and Cleena."

Bradach nodded to all of them. "I've only been here a day, but I've encountered so many rumors. It's hard to know what's the truth and what isn't."

"What have you heard?" Derry asked.

"That Usaeil is rarely at the castle anymore."

Cleena looked away when Bradach met her gaze. It was Felim who said, "It's a rare thing to see the queen about anymore. Some say that she isn't here, but others vow that she's locked away in her rooms, taking care of business."

"It would be nice to see her like we used to," Comgall said.

Derry nodded his head eagerly. "She used to walk among us, talking."

"What else have you heard?" Felim asked.

Bradach knew he'd won over the men, but Cleena was going to be more difficult. He wasn't giving up that easily, though. He had a suspicion that the female knew more than she was saying. "Well, there's one thing I know for a fact."

Comgall's eyes widened. "What is it?"

Everyone leaned forward, even Cleena. Bradach met each of their gazes before he said, "Usaeil has made movies with the humans. She's pretending to be mortal."

And to prove his story, Bradach used his magic to call up a copy of the magazine he and Maeve had found.

It was Cleena who snatched it out of his hand. She read the headline and took in Usaeil's picture plastered on the front before flipping to the pages where the article was. When she finished, she passed it on to Derry.

"I told you," she murmured.

Bradach seized his opportunity. "You knew she was doing this?"

Cleena glanced at him but didn't answer.

It was Comgall who released a loud sigh. "If Bradach was working for her, do you honestly believe he'd show us something like this?"

Bradach frowned and moved closer to the others as he lowered his voice. "You think there are spies among us?"

Cleena rolled her eyes. "Of course, there are. It began a few centuries ago, but with every decade, more and more spies move among us, listening to what we have to say and taking it back to Usaeil."

"You know this for certain?" Bradach pressed.

Felim's gaze dropped to the floor. "They took my wife away fifty years ago after she said something less than nice about the queen."

"We were all standing together, just like this," Derry said. "But she was the only one overheard."

Comgall nodded, his face set in grave lines. "We thought we'd all get questioned, but no one asked us a thing after they took her."

"But they're watching," Cleena said, her eyes narrowed on Bradach. "Always watching."

Bradach nodded as he glanced around him to see if anyone was listening. "There will always be someone unhappy with things. To try and control that is a disaster in the making."

"And breeds more discontent," Felim replied.

The rest nodded solemnly.

Bradach paused. The rumors he wanted to start would put others in danger, and he couldn't do that. He looked up and spotted Aisling, veiled, standing just behind Cleena. His fellow

Reaper must have just gotten there, but by her expression, she'd overheard the exchange between them.

After a moment, Aisling took a step back and shot him a wink. Bradach had no idea what she was going to do. Then, still veiled, she leaned close to three women who had their backs to her and whispered, "Usaeil has been masquerading as a movie star in the mortal world."

Just one whisper. That's all it took for the rumor to spread like wildfire throughout the court. No one knew who had begun it, which meant no one could be sent after them.

Bradach could practically watch the truth make its way through the court. And then his gaze landed on Maeve on the other side of the vast room. She smiled and gave him a wink.

CHAPTER
twenty

It was working! Maeve could barely contain her excitement. The entire great hall was abuzz with the news about Usaeil. And, suddenly, there were also copies of the human magazine with the queen on the cover circulating throughout the room.

Somehow, Bradach had achieved their goal. Maeve wasn't even upset that she hadn't been needed. She'd known that from the moment he asked her to go to the Light Castle. There was a look about Bradach that assured her that he could do anything on his own.

She'd wanted to help. And she had needed to deliver a blow to Usaeil. While she hadn't done anything, it was still nice to be a part of it. Even if just to see it all happening.

The smile on Maeve's face died when she spotted a group of people looking her way. For a heartbeat, she wondered if her glamour had slipped, but she knew that wasn't the case. Then someone pointed at her while talking to a tall, burly Queen's Guard member.

Maeve wanted to look behind her, but she kept her gaze straight ahead, pretending like she didn't know that someone was coming for her.

"Pssst."

Maeve kept calm while looking for a way to vanish before the Queen's Guard reached her. There were enough people that she might be able to do it, but it would have to be done soon.

"PSSST."

The sound was more persistent. She glanced to her side where the sound had come from to find a woman with long, black hair in dozens of braids standing behind a pillar. She waved Maeve over, but Maeve wasn't about to trust anyone but Bradach.

"Oh, for fek's sake," Maeve heard the woman mumble.

Maeve wished she hadn't come so far into the hall and away from the exits. She knew better than to make such a naïve move, but she hadn't been thinking of making a quick escape.

"If you want to live, come with me."

Maeve snapped her head in the direction of the woman. "Why are you helping me?"

"Because it's what Bradach wants."

At the mention of his name, Maeve felt her heart lurch. She had to get out of the castle, and she couldn't wait on him. Maeve had to make a decision. Remain and wait for the Queen's Guard to come for her, or leave with the unknown woman. Maeve knew she had a better chance with the woman.

Maeve waited until someone blocked the guard's view as he made his way through the throng of people, then Maeve ducked behind the column.

"Smart," the woman said. "I'm Aisling."

Maeve nodded and peered around the column to see if the guard was still coming. But she was quickly yanked back.

"Don't be stupid," Aisling snapped.

Maeve cut her eyes to the woman. "Do you have a way out?"

"There's a door about twenty feet to the left. Go through it. It'll take you down a corridor where you can get outside."

Maeve knew there was a good chance that this was all a trap. But what choice did she have?

Aisling rolled her eyes. "I'm not setting you up. Go, now."

She gave Maeve a little push to get moving. Maeve hurried to the doorway and quickly went through it, but she stopped and listened. To her surprise, when the guard reached Aisling, she told him that Maeve had left with two women.

Maeve leaned her head back against the wall for just a moment in dismay and delight. She hadn't been betrayed. Whoever Aisling was, maybe she really was working with Bradach. Maeve took a breath and began walking. The hallway was long. She tested every door she came to, but they were all locked. Finally, she found a window that allowed her to see outside. Surely, the door had to be close.

No sooner had the thought gone through her mind than she found it. Maeve walked from the castle. She half expected to see guards at the door, but there was no one. Almost as if Usaeil didn't think that anyone would be able to get away from her guards.

Maeve kept her pace even, and while she was out of the castle and able to teleport away, she didn't. She was waiting for the chance to see Bradach once more. They hadn't agreed to meet, but she'd assumed that they would by how he had spoken. And perhaps that was her weakness.

The hairs on the back of her neck prickled in warning. Every instinct she had alerted her to turn around and look behind her, but she kept her head straight. A few others were milling about the immense grounds, so she wasn't the only one outside.

She had gone another ten steps when she heard the sniffing. Her blood went cold, and her muscles locked. It was a sound she would never forget. One made by the beast that had nearly ended her life—and took Leon.

Maeve watched the others around her teleport away, fear flashing on their faces before they disappeared. She had bested a Tracker once. She could do so again.

Slowly, she turned to face the monstrosity. It stood about fifty feet from her, its milky gaze locked on her face. She thought of her father's favorite dagger. A moment later, it was in her hand.

Yet the Tracker didn't attack. It simply stared. It kept sniffing the air as if unsure of what it smelled.

In her peripheral, Maeve saw the castle. She thought of Bradach and how he'd achieved a step toward his goal. The talk about Usaeil would hurt the queen. Usaeil wouldn't be able to retaliate against anyone in particular, which would surely anger her.

Maeve still wasn't sure why she had been pointed out in the castle, but it didn't matter. It could have been anything she'd said or done. Bradach had cautioned her about court, and she knew from her time at the Dark Palace how cutthroat courtiers were. But she had allowed herself to be lulled into a sense of security at the Light Castle. And that was her mistake.

That was fine. She hadn't lied when she told Bradach she was prepared to give her life. She'd helped him, in what limited capacity she could. She might have won against the first Tracker, but this one looked . . . different. As if it knew she'd already bested one of the creatures. She might not make it out of this battle. That was too bad because she really wanted to be around to see the end result of Usaeil being taken down.

And to kiss Bradach one more time.

Aisling appeared out of nowhere, except there was now silver in her hair. Red eyes glanced toward Maeve, while Aisling's clothes changed from white to red and black to match her long, blood red nails.

Aisling eyed the Tracker before coming to stand beside Maeve. "Yeah, I'm Dark. Get over it."

"You should leave," Maeve told her. "It wants me."

Aisling smiled, her eyes never leaving the Tracker. "Did you not hear me inside? Bradach wants you kept safe."

"Why are you doing what he asks?"

"Because we're mates. It's what we do."

As if that explained everything. Maeve glanced at the Dark, thinking of everything Bradach had told her. If he was leery of the Dark, how was he friends with Aisling? That was obviously a question for later.

"I've killed one already. I'll take care of this one," Maeve told Aisling.

The Dark briefly cut her eyes to Maeve. "Sharing is caring. You had your fun. Let me have mine."

Maeve held up her hands. "You want him? Take him."

She took a step back when Aisling rushed the Tracker. The creature leaned out of the way and pushed the Dark to the ground as if she were nothing but a gnat to be flicked away. Then he advanced on Maeve.

Maeve spun and slashed with the long-bladed dagger when the Tracker got close enough. The nick did little but piss him off. Maeve turned again, this time in the other direction. But when she should've met flesh with the blade, there was nothing but air.

That barely registered before a fist connected with her cheek. Pain exploded on the side of her head as she flew through the air and landed heavily on the grass. The world spun viciously. Maeve tried to right herself, but it was taking far too long.

When she managed to push herself up to her hands and knees, she looked over to see Aisling fighting the Tracker. The Dark was quick—and very good—but the Tracker was nearly as fast. Maeve used the time to get her feet under her and find her blade again.

As soon as her hand wrapped around the weapon, the Tracker's eyes jerked to her. He forgot all about Aisling as he tossed the Dark aside like a rag doll.

Maeve was more prepared this time. Anger filled her as she imagined this Tracker being the one who had come to her home to take her people, to take the only friend Maeve had ever had. She would kill the beast for Leon.

She waited until the Tracker drew close, then she dodged and weaved and tried to get in as many jabs and slices with her blade as she could. She'd seen Aisling do it well, but for some reason, she couldn't seem to get the edge with this Tracker.

And then she realized why. He was anticipating her moves.

Even as she wondered how that was possible, the sun reflected off something metal around the Tracker's neck. Her gaze lowered to the necklace—an amulet that she recognized all too well. Her mouth fell open as she realized that she'd been battling Leon this entire time.

Shock reverberated through Maeve, causing her to still as she stared in horror at what was before her. The hesitation was a mistake because it allowed Leon time to wrap his fingers around her neck. She grasped his arm with her free hand and tried to get away, but he lifted her off the ground so that her feet dangled.

Their gazes locked. Maeve looked into his milky eyes for any sign of the Fae she'd known for centuries. But there was nothing.

"You . . . must . . . die," he said.

Maeve tried to get his name past her lips, but the pressure he exerted on her neck made it impossible. Black dots speckled her vision. She knew she was about to pass out, and then he would kill her.

Suddenly, Leon let out a bellow and released her. Maeve crumpled to the ground, coughing as she touched her throat. She looked up in time to see Leon turn, a sword protruding from his back, and Aisling smiling as she waited for him to advance.

"Wait!" Maeve tried to shout, but it came out as a croak. She swallowed and cleared her throat before she tried again. "Wait!"

Aisling ignored her, so Maeve jumped to her feet and got between the Dark and the Tracker. She met Leon's eyes, hoping to see some shred of the friend she'd known her entire life.

"Leon? Can you hear me?" she asked.

The Tracker peeled back his lips and laughed. "Leon is gone. I'm what's left."

"I don't believe you."

Behind her, Aisling snorted. "I'd believe it."

"Leon, it's me. Maeve," she tried again. "You're my friend. I gave you that necklace you're wearing."

As soon as she said it, Leon reached up and yanked the necklace off before throwing it aside. "I'm your enemy. I'm the one who's going to end your life."

"This isn't the real Leon talking." It couldn't be. This was Usaeil's magic.

Leon threw back his head and laughed. "Everything you have is because of me. If I hadn't killed your father, you'd still be hiding in your room, wondering what to do with your life."

Maeve blinked, utterly taken aback by his claims. She shook her head in disbelief. This couldn't be happening. The words coming out of his mouth weren't Leon's. They were Usaeil's. Weren't they?

And yet Usaeil hadn't been there when her father was murdered. It had been someone in the house. Maeve had investigated everyone. Everyone, that is, except Leon. Because she'd been sure that her dearest friend and closest confidant, the one who was like a brother to her, would never do such a thing.

How could Maeve absorb this news and accept it? Her father. The man who had shown her love and tenderness had been murdered by Leon.

A tear slipped down her face. "No."

"Oh, yes," Leon said with a wide smile, showing his fangs.

Any love she'd held for her friend vanished in that instant. She squared her shoulders, resolve taking firm hold of her.

And more realizations came. "You're the one who's been trying to kill me all these years."

"I nearly succeeded a couple of times," he snickered.

"But we trained together."

He shrugged half-heartedly. "You had some tricks up your sleeve that you kept even from me. That's the only reason you've survived. That, and luck."

She shook her head. "My skill has nothing to do with luck."

Maeve tightened her hand on her father's blade right before she attacked. She moved faster than she ever had, falling back to her first lessons in combat with her father.

She stayed just out of Leon's reach, going in to make a cut and moving back out. Again and again and again, she repeated the process, slicing him on his Achilles tendon and behind the knee as well as on his upper body.

It wasn't long before blood seeped from all his wounds to coat him. It fell into the grass, causing him to slip. There was so much of it that it also caused Maeve to lose her footing, but she recovered quickly.

But not swiftly enough, as Leon's hand clamped around her throat once more.

She waited until he lifted her to eye level with him. Then, while he smiled in triumph, Maeve shoved her father's blade into the side of his throat.

The sight of Leon gripping Maeve by the throat triggered a tightness in Bradach's chest that felt as if the weight of the entire realm rested on him. He was so engrossed in the battle that he forgot that Eoghan and Cathal held him back.

"Get off me," he ground out to them, his gaze locked on the woman who captivated him.

"Wait," Cathal said.

Bradach tried to jerk his arm free. "No."

"She has to do this on her own," Eoghan stated.

Bradach glanced at him, confused and angry. "You can't be serious."

But Eoghan was.

Then Maeve plunged the blade into Leon's throat.

Relief surged through Bradach, but it didn't diminish his ire at his friends. He realized then that Eoghan and Cathal had used their veil to hide him from Maeve. He glared at them, waiting for them to release him. As soon as they did, the veil fell away from him. He took a step toward Maeve as she stood looking down at her former friend. Bradach didn't know what to say to her.

She'd just learned that the only person she'd ever trusted had betrayed her from the beginning. No matter how much Bradach searched his mind, there weren't words that could convey his sorrow for her discovery or the rage at what had been done to her.

Out of the corner of his eye, Bradach saw Aisling look his way. The other five Reapers remained veiled as they stood in a circle around them. Bradach had witnessed the entire battle. From the moment Maeve had left the castle, he'd been there.

He'd tried to go to her, but Eoghan and the others had held him back, preventing him from going to help. All he could think about was the Tracker killing her. But, somehow, Eoghan had known differently.

"Wait. Watch," Eoghan had whispered.

That was the last thing Bradach had wanted. And yet, in the end, he'd seen the extent of Maeve's skill in battle. Her movements were nearly as quick as a Reaper's, but it was her ferocity that excited him.

She'd wanted to help Leon, but the moment Maeve realized that it was either her life or his, her entire demeanor had changed. He would expect it from someone who had seen years of combat. But it proved that some were born for battle.

Maeve's gaze lifted to him. The smile that pulled at her lips had him grinning like a fool. But in an instant, the smile vanished, replaced by a frown as she cocked her head to the side. Her eyes slid to Aisling before Maeve returned her attention to Bradach.

He swallowed, unease slithering through him. He took a tentative step in her direction. "I'm sorry about Leon."

Aisling rolled her eyes and shook her head. But it was the way

Maeve visibly straightened her back that made him realize that he'd said the wrong thing.

"You knew this was Leon?" Maeve asked, pointing to the dead Tracker.

There was no way he could take back his words, so Bradach just nodded his head.

"The only other person in this battle was Aisling. How do you know about Leon?"

Bradach knew there was no way for him to come out of this without lying. And he didn't want to do that. Not to Maeve. But he also couldn't tell her the truth. It would mean her instant death, and he refused to let that happen.

If he couldn't lie to her, then that left him with nothing. So, he remained silent.

The pain that flashed across her face was like a punch to Bradach's gut. She took a step back, putting distance between them. Bradach wanted to reach for her, to stop her. But he knew it was futile. He'd lost her the moment he couldn't give her an answer.

Actually, he'd never had her.

That's what hurt the worst. Because, for just a little while, Bradach had allowed himself to believe that he could have Maeve. That they could have . . . something.

She took another few steps back. Any moment now, she'd teleport away. It would be the last time Bradach saw her. Moments of their interlude that had passed entirely too quickly flashed in his mind. The softness of her skin, her sensual response to his touch, the way she drove him mad with need.

Bradach thought of Eoghan and the other set of Reapers. Each one of them had been in a similar situation. Somehow, all of them had been able to come out ahead because the women had been

Halflings. The only Fae wife was Neve, who was now a Reaper herself.

Maeve didn't fit into either of those categories, which left Bradach with nothing. He didn't dare test the waters by telling her the truth because he wouldn't be able to handle it if Death appeared and killed Maeve.

Bradach had to admit that he now understood why Bran had lashed out as he had. He'd watched the love of his life be taken away for breaking a rule.

While Bradach might be losing Maeve, at least she still had her life. That was something.

With every step Maeve took away from him, the happiness that Bradach had found in her arms slipped away, bit by bit like sand falling from his hand. There would be nothing left when she was gone. He'd thought he'd been a shell of a person before, but he'd only had a taste of it. He was about to learn what it truly meant to lose someone he loved.

Bradach gasped, his lips parting as he struggled to breathe. By the stars! He loved her. He loved her!

And he was letting her go.

All the words he wanted to say but couldn't filled his head. They lodged in his throat, cutting off his air and leaving the bitter taste of regret and grief behind.

The sudden appearance of twelve Trackers circling them caught even Maeve's attention. She halted and swiveled her head to take in the dozen creatures. Immediately, she shifted and headed back toward Bradach.

He knew it wasn't because she wanted to be with him, but that didn't matter. She was still there. That's what counted. Or so he thought. That changed the instant Aisling looked his way and shook her head.

Bradach frowned and tried to teleport to get behind one of the Trackers, but something held him back. If he pushed harder, he might be able to do it, but then it would let whoever had put up the shield know that he was powerful enough to break through it.

When Maeve twirled the large blade in her hand, Bradach smiled. She could take care of herself. She'd proven that twice already. That didn't mean he wouldn't stay near her. Just in case.

Bradach turned in a circle, looking at each of the Trackers. He raised a brow when all they did was look at him. "Which one of you is going to talk?"

It was one behind him that gave a loud snort. Bradach turned to find the Tracker's milky eyes gazing at him with derision. "There's no need to converse. We're here for her."

The tightness in Bradach's chest was back when the creature pointed at Maeve. Even though he'd known that the Trackers were there for her, hearing one of them state it was completely different.

"Leave," the Tracker told Bradach and Aisling.

Aisling flicked one of her many long braids over a shoulder. "You obviously have no idea who I am if you say that."

The Tracker grinned. "Good. Another to kill."

Bradach liked that the others ignored him. He hadn't said anything, so the Trackers assumed he would stay out of the fight. That was their mistake.

He looked between two Trackers to Dubhan who was still veiled along with the rest of the Reapers. Bradach wasn't worried about the beasts or the fact that it appeared as if the fight were three against twelve.

What concerned him was that he wouldn't be able to fight as he usually did as a Reaper. He was all too aware of the fact that there were hundreds, if not thousands of Fae eyes watching from the castle windows.

Bradach found himself standing between Maeve and Aisling. The time for talking was over. It was now time for battle.

"You ready?" Aisling asked.

Bradach didn't take his eyes from the Trackers. "Absolutely."

"I'm going to shield us so that no one else can see."

Bradach frowned and glanced at her. Aisling's grin let him know that she meant the Reapers, not just the three of them. He laughed, which confused the Trackers.

Aisling wiggled her fingers, showing off her long, red nails. "It's not nice to keep a lady waiting. What are you ugly tossers waiting for? An invitation? Well, here it is," she said sarcastically.

The nearest Tracker rushed her. Maeve moved to help Aisling, but Bradach stopped her and whispered, "Wait."

In just two moves, the creature lay dead at Aisling's feet.

"Impressive," Maeve said beneath her breath.

Aisling flashed her a smile. "I knew I liked you."

"Kill them!" the first Tracker bellowed.

As one, the eleven rushed them. No sooner did that happen than the other Reapers dropped their veils and attacked. Bradach stayed near Maeve, but he let her fight her own battle. He kept his eye on her as he finished off a Tracker. As he went for his second kill, Rordan threw one of his knives, burying it in the creature's skull.

The skirmish was over quickly. Maeve wiped her forehead with the back of her arm and cleaned off the blood from her blade before it disappeared.

She didn't say anything about the appearance of the other five Fae, but Bradach knew that she'd noticed them. Perhaps he shouldn't leave it to her to ask.

"Bloody hell, you're good," Aisling said as she walked to Maeve.

Maeve smiled. "Thanks. I've trained most of my life for those trying to take me out. I never thought I'd be using such skills against something like this."

Bradach tore his gaze from Maeve since she wouldn't look his way and found himself staring into quicksilver eyes. Eoghan gave a single nod of his head. Bradach knew his leader was giving him permission to tell Maeve everything, but it was easier said than done.

Aisling bent and retrieved the blade from the Tracker's skull and returned it to Rordan. The six Reapers stood in a group facing Bradach and Maeve. Bradach felt as if he were under a microscope. It was uncomfortable and irritating.

"I think we should leave," Eoghan finally said into the silence.

The six picked up two Trackers each and teleported away one by one. Aisling was the last. She gave Bradach a wink. With her departure, the shield keeping them hidden from the castle was gone.

Bradach cleared his throat as the others from the castle saw him once more. He turned to Maeve. "I suppose you have questions."

"No," Maeve said quickly.

"I couldn't tell you before. I can now."

She spun to look at him. "I don't want to know."

He wasn't prepared for the resentment he heard in her voice or the look he saw in her eyes. "Maeve, please."

"I knew it was wrong for us to be together, but I ignored my instincts. And what has it gotten me?" she asked with a harsh bark of laughter. "Not a bloody thing."

Bradach had remained silent before. He wasn't going to now. "I knew about Leon because I was veiled."

The look she gave him could have flayed him alive. "I figured that out since I already knew you could do that."

"The others can, as well."

"I told you I don't want to know."

He moved to stand before her, blocking her from leaving. "I tried to help you with the Tracker, but they held me back."

"Waiting for me to get killed so I'd no longer be a problem."

"What?" he asked in confusion. Then he shook his head. "No. Eoghan knew you could take the Tracker on your own, and he wanted me to see it. We're good at what we do, so we recognize it in others."

"That's nice." Maeve pivoted to the side and walked around him.

Bradach spun and hurried to catch up to her. "I don't want you to go."

"That's too bad."

"Please. Talk to me."

She kept walking, refusing to look at him. "I've nothing to say."

Bradach halted, hating himself for the fact that he could only come up with one thing that might make her stay. He didn't want to use it, but he couldn't let her leave. "Usaeil won't stop trying to kill you. She'll send more and more Trackers."

Maeve stopped walking. She drew in a deep breath that caused her shoulders to rise. Only then did she turn to him. "And I told you, everything must die eventually."

Before the last syllable was out of her mouth, she teleported away. Leaving Bradach all alone with an ache in his chest that he knew would never dissipate.

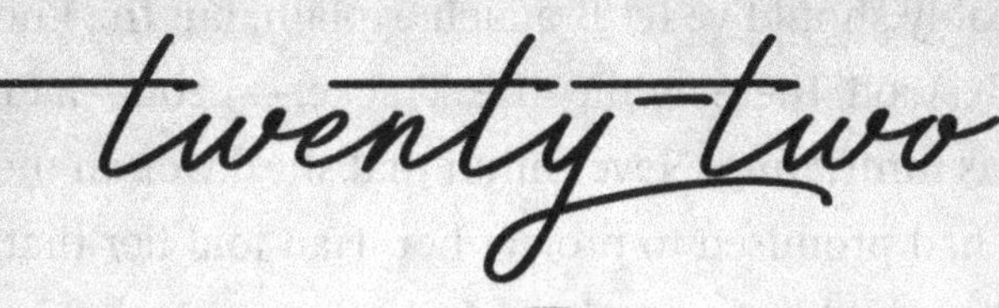

CHAPTER twenty-two

Maeve was such a fool. Such an absolute, total fool.

And yet, the moment she left Bradach, all she wanted to do was return to him.

She blinked to clear her eyes that had suddenly gone fuzzy, only to realize she was crying. Crying! She wasn't someone who let emotion get to her on such a level, but there was no stopping it this time.

Maeve stood in the middle of her bedroom. There was nowhere else for her to go. Nor was there anyone for her to go to. She'd spent a lifetime secluding herself from anyone who might hurt her. And look where that had gotten her.

Her best friend, the brother she'd never had, had turned out to be a traitor and a murderer. Maeve's carefully constructed life was in utter shambles. Everything she'd worked so hard for was gone. Her enemies would soon swoop in to pick apart her empire.

And she didn't care.

Her heart was broken, shattered. She'd made the ultimate mistake—she'd fallen in love.

With a Fae she couldn't have.

She probably should've let Bradach explain, but the knowledge that he had stood there while the Tracker—Leon—had nearly killed her was infuriating. Never mind that she'd won in the end.

Bradach had promised to protect her. Had told her that no one would hurt her. And Leon nearly had.

You bested Leon. Your ego is bruised, that's all.

It was more than her ego. It was her heart, her trust. She had believed that Bradach would hold to his word. It shouldn't matter that he hadn't, but it did.

She wandered about her chamber while thinking of Bradach, Aisling, and the other five Fae who had suddenly appeared. They'd all fought with such intensity that Maeve wanted to see more of it —and ask them to train her.

The group was Bradach's secret. They obviously held influence in order to get the King of the Dark to help them, especially since they were a mix of Light and Dark Fae.

Maeve put her hand over her heart. She was numb. Perhaps a more apt word would be heartbroken. She closed her eyes, and a mental image of Bradach filled her mind. He was everything special and good that had come into her life. She'd thrown caution to the wind and followed her heart for the first time ever. She'd known he had a secret, and it hadn't bothered her. She'd told him as much.

Why did it now?

Because he watched as you fought Leon.

Was she really going to allow something so . . . trivial . . . to keep her from him? Or was she using that as an excuse to close herself off from the overwhelming and amazing feelings that had developed between them?

Maeve opened her eyes. She wasn't sure how long she had before Usaeil sent more Trackers after her. One on one, she could hold her own. But more than that? Maeve really didn't want to find out.

She immediately returned to the Light Castle in the hopes that Bradach was still there. What she found were dozens of Fae milling about the area where the battle had taken place. She heard them talking about the creatures, but before anyone noticed her, she teleported away.

This time, she went to the only other place she could think of—the Dark Palace. She put up her glamour and made her way inside, but Maeve didn't seek out Balladyn. She really didn't know what she was doing there. The king wasn't exactly a friend. She'd made sure not to have any of those.

Maeve wandered the main level of the stronghold. She watched the depravity of the Dark with the humans they had sex with, draining their souls in the process. She overheard conversations about betrayal and murder, and she couldn't help but compare it to the Light Castle.

No one paid her any heed. Here, she was an outsider. Court life was a whole other beast that she'd never cared to learn. Though, in truth, it wasn't much different than navigating the waters of business. Both had backstabbers and traitors and murderers.

Dealing with business was enough for her. She'd never felt the need to be immersed in court, as well.

Suddenly, she realized she was being watched. Maeve slowly swiveled her head, searching for whoever was observing her, when she spotted Balladyn at the top of the stairs. He leaned one shoulder against a giant pillar, his arms folded over his chest, one ankle crossed over the other. He lifted a brow. It was all the summons she needed.

Maeve took a deep breath and released it as she pivoted and made her way to the stairs. She ascended them, noting that guards silently took up residence at the bottom behind her.

She reached Balladyn and stood next to him, looking down at the others. Both she and the king were silent. She didn't know what was on Balladyn's mind, but she was aware of more guards stealthily moving in to take their positions.

If that was on the main floor, she assumed there were more on the others, as well. Balladyn would only do that if he thought there was a threat. That must mean the king knew about the Trackers.

"The comparisons between the palace and the castle are many," Balladyn finally said.

She swung her head to him. So, he knew she'd gone to the Light Castle. "Yes."

"It's a beautiful place."

Did she hear some forlornness in his voice? The castle had been his home once. "It is. But so is this palace."

Balladyn's red eyes met hers. "In an entirely different way."

"It all depends on the eye of the beholder."

One side of the king's lips turned up in a grin. "And which do you prefer?"

Was this a trick? Had Bradach told Balladyn her secret? As soon as the thought went through her mind, she knew it was ridiculous. "There are parts of both I like."

"Aye," Balladyn said solemnly and turned his head away. "You have a powerful enemy."

Maeve pressed her lips together. "How did you find out?"

"I knew the moment you agreed to help Bradach that the odds of Usaeil discovering you aiding him were great."

"And you didn't caution me?"

He grunted and glanced at her. "Would you have listened?"

In truth, no, she wouldn't have. She turned her attention back to those below her. Many looked in her and Balladyn's direction, but none dared to venture too close.

"Usaeil is my enemy, as well," Balladyn said. "She has been so for some time. I aided Bradach and the others recently, and I will continue doing so."

"Because it helps rid you of a foe."

The king straightened, dropping his arms to his sides as he faced her. "That is a benefit, aye, but I also do it because of who Bradach is. I know about the battle at the castle, as well as the Trackers after you."

Maeve straightened her back. "Is this where you ask me to leave?"

"If I wanted you gone, I would've made sure you could never enter the palace in the first place. Follow me," he ordered.

It never entered her mind not to do as he bade. Maeve trailed behind Balladyn up more stairs and finally to his chambers. He didn't speak again until the doors had closed behind them, sealing them off from the guards on the other side.

"I didn't come here to seek your help," she said. "I don't actually know why I came. I know that I put you and everyone else in danger because the Trackers will come."

Balladyn didn't look at her as he poured whisky into two tumblers and brought one to her. He shrugged and took a drink. "It doesn't matter why you came, though I'm glad you did."

That made her frown. "Why?"

"Because on some level, you trust me." He flashed her a quick grin. "I like you. And I'm not the only one."

"Meaning?" she asked before taking a drink. She savored the whisky on her tongue before she let it slide down her throat.

"You made quite an impression on not just Bradach, but on his associates, as well."

She shrugged. "What does that mean?"

"It means that you're not alone."

If Maeve thought she had her emotions under control, she discovered with just one sentence that tears threatened once more. She hastily blinked and looked away.

Balladyn walked to one of the chairs in the middle of the room and sat. "All you have to do is say his name."

"That sounds easy," Maeve murmured.

"Because it is." Balladyn set the tumbler down on the table next to him. "It's easy to build walls and shut yourself away. Trust me, I know. I've done it from the moment I woke up in the dungeons below us."

Her head snapped to him. Maeve knew Balladyn sharing even a little of his past wasn't normal. "The walls are safe."

"Are they?" he asked. His red eyes took on a faraway look. "I used to think so, but not anymore." Balladyn was silent for a heartbeat before he blinked and focused his gaze on her again. "If you go this alone, you might evade the Trackers for a while, but eventually, they'll find you."

She swallowed. "And if I don't do this alone?"

"Then you'll survive."

Three words. That's all it took for her to realize that she held the keys to not just her future but her happiness, as well. Whether she ended up with Bradach or not, she was the only one able to make the decision on which direction to take.

Balladyn smiled then and waved his hand, revealing a Fae doorway that had been hidden. "Good luck, Maeve. I foresee us meeting on the battlefield soon to face our mutual foe."

Maeve finished the whisky and set the glass down. "Thank you, my king. It'll be an honor to stand with you. Anytime."

Maeve hurried through the doorway and found herself in the middle of Dublin. She didn't call for Bradach, though. Instead, she said, "Aisling."

twenty-three

"Well, I didn't expect this."

Maeve inwardly winced at the anger flashing in Aisling's red eyes. "Thank you for coming."

"Why call for me?" the Dark demanded.

Maeve licked her lips. "A couple of reasons. One, I wanted to thank you again for helping me. I know you didn't do it because you wanted to, but I still owe you."

Aisling looked at a long, red nail. "You don't owe me anything. I took great pleasure in killing the Trackers."

This wasn't going well, but then again, Maeve hadn't really expected it to. "I overreacted with Bradach. I want to explain it to him."

"Then call for him," Aisling said as she lowered her hand. There were no longer sparks in her gaze.

Maeve glanced at the ground. "I will. I—I'm working up to it."

"Never done this before, have you?" Aisling asked, a grin playing about her lips.

A nervous laugh left Maeve. "Never."

"Don't overthink it. Just say what's in your heart."

"If he comes."

Aisling rolled her eyes. "He'll come."

"Really?" It wasn't until that moment that Maeve realized how terrified she was that Bradach would want nothing to do with her.

Aisling walked to Maeve's side and threw an arm around her shoulder. "Oh, this is going to be fun. I had no idea you didn't know how to traverse the murky, dangerous waters of relationships."

"I don't know what I have with Bradach."

"It's in the beginning stages," Aisling replied. "Think of it as an infant. It needs lots of attention and love for it to grow."

Maeve felt a knot growing in her stomach. The anxiety increased the longer she stood there, thinking about all the things she wanted to say to Bradach. "I walked away from him. Left him."

"Arguments and disagreements are a part of life. Trust me. It's how you deal with the aftermath that makes or breaks a relationship, be it romantic or with friends."

Maeve looked at the Dark as a lightbulb went off in her head. "It's like a business deal."

Aisling looked skyward and tilted her head back and forth a few times as she twisted her lips. "Yeah. That's a good analogy for you."

"That makes things a little easier."

"Good." Aisling moved to stand in front of Maeve. "Just say whatever is in your heart. You can't go wrong if you do that. And, don't forget to apologize."

Maeve nodded, smiling. "Right."

"Good luck."

And to Maeve's surprise, Aisling leaned forward and gave her a quick hug before vanishing.

Maeve took a deep breath and whispered, "Bradach."

Her heart slammed against her ribs as she waited, expectantly. Yet, with every second that passed and he didn't arrive, melancholy set in.

Maeve couldn't even be upset. She was the one who hadn't listened to him. She was the one who'd left. What did she expect? That he'd come running back to her if she called?

She couldn't stand there for another moment. She needed to walk, or . . . something. Since there was nowhere for her to go, she'd just walk the city as she tried to formulate a plan for her future.

Maeve turned on her heel, her gaze landing on the figure in all black standing behind her. She jerked as Usaeil's red lips turned up in a malevolent smile.

"You look upset," Usaeil said mockingly as her silver eyes shifted to red. "Something wrong? Why not share all the details with me?"

Maeve let the surprise rush through her before she tucked it away. This was where she would die, but she wasn't going down without landing some punches of her own.

Usaeil looked around as if nothing were wrong. "No one can see us or hear us. I've made sure of that."

"Yes, you wouldn't want the humans to see you for who you really are."

"Oh, ho," Usaeil replied with a bark of laughter. "There's Maeve the Merciless. But I think you can do better than that."

Maeve raked her gaze scornfully over the queen. "Come to do your own dirty work, have you?"

"Unlike you, who sends others to do it for you."

They slowly circled each other. Maeve knew she didn't have the magic to compete with Usaeil, but she hadn't been raised to back down from anyone. Not even someone like the queen.

Balladyn had said that she wasn't alone, but the proof was before her. Maeve had always been alone. From the moment of her birth, it had just been her. There were a few people who came and went in her life, but in the end, it was always her. Alone.

Usaeil lips turned into a sneer. "The Reapers, Maeve? Really? I can't believe you would stoop to helping them."

It felt as if the ground fell out from under Maeve's feet. Reapers. Surely, Usaeil had to be wrong. And yet. . . .

The queen continued talking, unaware of Maeve's shock. "They're not as powerful as they lead everyone to believe. It wasn't that long ago that I met Death herself. In my chambers at the Light Castle, in fact." Usaeil stopped walking and laughed loudly. "She and the Reapers had a chance to take me down, but they didn't. I realized then that they don't have what it takes. No one can best me. No one."

Maeve lifted her chin. "If there's one thing I've learned from being on top, it's that it doesn't matter how much power or influence or magic you have. There will always be someone who will topple you."

"Not for me," Usaeil declared.

"To think that at one time I respected you. Now all I feel is contempt."

Usaeil rolled her eyes dramatically before saying sarcastically, "Oh, how your words wound."

"If we're going to fight, then let's get on with it."

"So ready to die, are you?"

Maeve called her father's dagger to her as well as her favorite sword. With a weapon in each hand, she sized up her enemy.

Usaeil was powerful, but she was also over-confident. Maeve preferred to be on the offense rather than the defense, so she attacked first.

To her delight, the blade of her sword made contact with Usaeil's arm, cutting through fabric and skin to draw blood.

The queen looked at the injury before sliding her gaze to Maeve. "That will be the first and last time you draw my blood."

Maeve equalized her footing right before Usaeil advanced. The queen came at her with weapons and magic. Maeve dodged the majority of the attack, but several balls of power struck her. She knew Dark magic well, but that's not what burned through her skin. This was something different, something darker. More sinister.

Maeve spun, ignoring the pain crippling her body as she lifted her sword in time to block a swing from Usaeil's blade. Maeve pushed the queen away before flipping backwards, letting the toe of her shoe catch Usaeil on the chin.

Maeve landed and saw the queen stumble back a few steps, wiping blood from her lip. "Looks like I drew more blood."

"You got lucky."

Maeve grinned. "You sure it's just luck? Or are you losing your touch? Perhaps it's because your people are learning who you really are."

Usaeil drew up short. "What's that supposed to mean?"

"Perhaps you should spend more time at your castle."

Hate and fury burned in Usaeil's now blood red eyes. "What have you done?"

Maeve didn't answer, she just smiled.

Usaeil lifted her sword, pointing the end of the blade at Maeve. "This isn't over. I will find you."

"I'm not running."

In the next breath, Usaeil was gone. Humans near Maeve gave her strange looks. That's when she realized that the spell to hide them was gone. She hid her weapons and turned as fear settled around her like a cold, wet blanket.

She'd been given a reprieve. It would most likely be a short one, but she wasn't going to let it go to waste. If she had to search the entire realm, she would find Bradach and admit she'd been wrong. She would tell him that she shouldn't have walked away.

Her eyes closed as she thought of him. How she wished he was there so she could step into his arms and have him hold her. That's all she needed. Just to be held.

"Bradach," she called.

She knew he wouldn't come, but she had to repeat his name. If only she hadn't been so stupid. If only she'd realized just how much he meant to her before it was too late. If only. . . .

Regret wasn't something she could live with. Somehow, some-way, Maeve would tell Bradach all the things she hadn't been able to. It didn't matter what he was. Fae or Reaper or something alto-gether different. She had fallen hard and fast for him.

Something touched her cheek. The caress was soft, sensual. A hand then fell to her shoulder and ran down her arm to her waist. Then she was pulled forward, and strong arms came around her.

Without having to look, she knew it was Bradach. She wound her arms around him and clung to him as if he were life—because he was.

"I'm here," he whispered.

Maeve wanted to stay just where she was, her cheek resting on his chest. But some things needed to be said. "I should've let you talk."

"You had every right to be upset."

She shook her head and leaned back to look at him. "I was

scared by how close I came to dying, and I blamed you for not helping me. That wasn't fair."

"Maeve, I—"

She put a hand over his lips to stop him and smiled softly. "Please, let me finish. I didn't expect to trust you, but I did. You brought excitement into my very dull life. You showed me pleasure and desire, as well as danger. And I loved every second of it. I was a fool to walk away. I'm sorry."

Bradach gently pulled her hand away. "There's nothing to apologize for. I was going to tell you who I am."

"A Reaper."

His brows snapped together. "How did you guess?"

"I didn't." She swallowed. "Usaeil was here. She told me."

Bradach looked around, his gaze searching every face for the queen. "When? Where?"

"Just a few minutes before you arrived. She wanted to kill me herself."

His eyes snapped back to her. "Did you kill her?"

"No," Maeve said with a shake of her head. "I drew blood, though. Twice."

He smiled widely. "That's my girl."

"I told her she might want to check on her people because they were learning about her. That was enough to get her to leave. For now. She'll be back for me."

Bradach took Maeve's hand and led her to an alley. Then he faced her. "I am a Reaper. I couldn't tell you because any Fae who knows of us dies."

"And yet, Usaeil is still alive." Maeve gave a shake of her head. "The stories I was told were about how powerful the Reapers are."

"That isn't a lie."

"Then how is Usaeil still alive?"

Bradach ran a hand down his face. "It's complicated. Death could judge Usaeil, but she is waiting."

"On what?"

Bradach blew out a long breath. "It's someone else's destiny to kill Usaeil."

"Sooooooo. You work for Death, huh?"

"Remember when I said I had been murdered?"

Maeve nodded.

"Death saw it all. After I died, she gave me an option. Remain dead, or have her grant me life and become one of her Reapers."

"I have to admit," Maeve said, looking him up and down. "That's pretty hot."

twenty-four

Bradach was glad there wasn't fear in Maeve's eyes. Instead, there was admiration and approval. If he'd had any doubts before about whether or not he and Maeve belonged together, all of them vanished right then.

"I know why Death chose you," Maeve said. "You're not just a skilled warrior, you're a good man. The best."

He gave a shake of his head. "I'm not perfect. I have faults."

"And the fact you can admit that proves my point."

Bradach couldn't believe that she was in his life. Maeve was everything he'd despised, and yet, she was now everything he needed and loved. He'd never imagined that he would freely give a Dark his heart.

"I love you." There were many ways he'd imagined telling Maeve of his feelings, but he forgot each and every one. In the end, he decided on the basic truth.

She reached up and touched his cheek. His heart thudded in his chest. He'd never told a woman that he loved them before. He wasn't even sure if she felt the same about him, but it didn't matter. It was important that Maeve know of his feelings, that he wanted to be with her.

"I love you," she replied in a soft voice. Then her lips curved into a smile.

For a moment, Bradach couldn't breathe. He wasn't sure if Maeve had actually said the words aloud or if his brain had heard what he wanted to hear. But the look in her eyes confirmed the truth.

He threw his arms around her, yanking her tightly against him. But his elation was dimmed because he wasn't sure what kind of future they could have together.

Everything about his and Maeve's relationship was vastly different from any other Reaper's. And while Death might have consented to Reapers having significant others, he would be the first going to her to ask . . . well, he didn't know what exactly.

"What is it?" Maeve asked as she leaned back to look at him.

"Until recently, the Reapers weren't allowed to have relationships with anyone. When we take Death's offer to live again, we leave behind our lives and the people we knew."

Maeve's smile was a little tight as she nodded. "The simple fact that there isn't a lot of knowledge about the Reapers says how well all of you have kept things together."

"Things are changing. Before, anyone who wasn't a Reaper and knew of us was killed."

"Balladyn knows who you are."

"That he does. Death is the one who gave him the information. Though, to be fair, he'd worked a few things out on his own when he met Fintan, another Reaper. Death gave Balladyn the knowledge and then asked him to fight alongside her."

Maeve tucked her hair behind her ear. "Which he did. And he's still alive."

"Yes."

"But you're worried about me."

Bradach couldn't deny it. "Eoghan urged me to tell you who I was. He wouldn't have done that without knowing how things would go with Death."

"I see the worry in your eyes," Maeve stated.

"It's not just Death. It's Usaeil that concerns me."

Maeve lifted her shoulders nonchalantly. "From the moment I took over my father's business, I've had people after me. I've survived for thousands of years. I'm not easy to kill."

Bradach tried to smile at her jest, but he couldn't manage it. "I can't lose you."

"You won't."

But they both knew it could happen in an instant. Especially with the Trackers.

Maeve licked her lips and ran her hands over his shoulders. "So, what does being a Reaper entail exactly?"

"Death passes judgment, and we collect the souls of the Fae."

"I've seen the way all of you move. You're quick."

He couldn't help himself, Bradach had to have a kiss. He pressed his lips against hers, lingering for just a moment. "When we become Reapers, we're given added magic and power."

"Making you stronger than the average Fae. That would make you nearly as strong as both Balladyn and Usaeil. Why then does the queen believe she's stronger than all of you? Even Death?"

Bradach pulled away until only their hands were linked. "Because we gave her that impression. We had a chance to kill her but didn't."

"Why would you do that?" Maeve asked, shock causing her face to go slack.

"If there's one thing you should know, it's that Death is more powerful than any other being on this realm. In fact, I doubt any in the universe can match her. She was once known as the Mistress of War."

"Truly? Then I don't understand why she would allow Usaeil to continue."

Bradach flashed her a quick grin. "It's a question I ask every day. All I can say is that Death believes that Usaeil's life needs to be taken by someone else."

"Then I'll take it," Maeve offered.

His brave, brilliant woman. Bradach's heart swelled with pride that she was his. "It's not that simple. There is someone Death has already stated shall do the deed."

"That's great. Why aren't they doing it?"

"I believe it's all going to happen very soon, but we're not the only ones after the queen."

Maeve nodded. "Right. Balladyn."

"There is also the Dragon Kings."

Her eyes widened. "Usaeil certainly gets around pissing people off, doesn't she?"

"She's a master at it."

"You started all this looking for Xaneth, and you're no closer to finding him."

Bradach blew out a breath. "He's not the only one Usaeil took. She also has the King of Dragon Kings."

"Constantine." Maeve whistled softly. "No wonder the Kings want a piece of her."

"It's going to get rough."

"I don't care. I'll stand by you, fight with you until my last breath."

Bradach leaned forward to kiss Maeve, but she was suddenly gone. He glanced hastily around, looking for Trackers or Usaeil. Then his gaze landed on Cael.

The Reaper leader's dark purple eyes held his. "Easy, Bradach."

"Where is Maeve?" he demanded, advancing on Cael. He didn't care that Cael now had as much power as Erith. All Bradach wanted was his woman.

Cael held up his hands and kept his voice even. "Death wanted to talk to her."

"She could've done it here. With me!" Bradach closed his eyes and turned away. If Erith hurt her. . . .

"Do you really believe that Death would allow Reapers to have relationships only to revoke it for you?"

Bradach opened his eyes. He ran a hand through his hair. "I don't know."

"It takes a special kind of person to love one of us. We aren't typical Fae, Bradach. You know this."

"Maeve isn't average either."

Cael nodded, his lips curving in a slight smile. "I saw."

"Saw?" Bradach asked in shock.

"Yes. Maeve is extremely skilled as a fighter. She proved her worth several times, but more importantly, she demonstrated her nobility and character in multiple ways."

Some of the anxiety left Bradach. "You make it sound as if you like her."

"I do," Cael admitted. "But I'm not the one who needs to be convinced. Erith is."

Bradach's apprehension doubled. "I love Maeve more than I thought anyone could love anything. She is my heart, my soul."

Cael moved forward and placed his hand on Bradach's shoulder. "Each individual must prove themselves to the Reaper they love, to the leaders, and to Death. We've all been betrayed. Erith wants to make sure that doesn't happen again."

"Maeve wouldn't."

"Trust in your love for her."

But all Bradach could think about was not having Maeve in his life. It felt as if he were tumbling through an abyss as he reached for her in the darkness.

Cael dropped his arm to his side. "It's time for you to return home. Your mission is finished."

"What about Xaneth?"

"We'll continue searching for him, but the war against Usaeil is starting. We need to be ready."

With that, Cael vanished. Bradach waited a few more minutes, hoping that Maeve would return, but he teleported to the tiny island in the middle of a Scottish loch before he stepped through the doorway that took him to Death's realm—or the Reapers' realm now.

As soon as he was through, his gaze found the soaring white tower through the thick foliage. Was Maeve there? No, Erith wouldn't bring anyone there who wasn't a part of their group.

Bradach spotted Cathal and Rordan walking toward the newly constructed building that was their meeting center. He had no wish to see anyone, so he teleported to the top of the mountain he'd been standing on when Eoghan informed him of his mission.

The sun was sinking into the horizon. Bradach fisted his hands. So many times, Maeve had come close to dying, and somehow, she'd made it through each one. It felt as if it had been fated for them to meet.

A few days ago, he'd have laughed at the idea. But not now.

Especially when he thought about how Eoghan could have sent any Reaper to find Maeve. He'd sent Bradach.

And Bradach had fallen head over heels for not just any Dark, but Maeve the Merciless. He smiled.

One minute, Maeve was looking at Bradach. The next, she was staring into the face of a being so beautiful it barely registered. She blinked, unnerved by the lavender eyes gazing at her.

"Hello, Maeve," the woman said.

Without needing to be told, Maeve knew this was Death. She'd never thought to put a face to the being. She'd always just thought of Death as an entity, a spirit. Now, she found herself face-to-face with a petite woman with long, wavy black hair wearing black pants and an armored corset as well as matching gauntlets.

Mistress of War or Death, both titles fit the woman perfectly.

Maeve swallowed, just now realizing that they were in the empty castle she called home. The ballroom looked huge compared to a few days ago when she hosted the party. "Hello."

"You know who I am?"

Maeve nodded. "Death."

A black brow arched. "You don't seem afraid."

"Just because I don't show it doesn't mean I don't feel it."

Death smiled, her gaze holding Maeve's. "Well said."

Maeve held back a shiver of fear. It couldn't be a good sign that Death had taken her from Bradach. "Please don't punish Bradach."

"You believe I brought you here because I intend to punish Bradach?"

"He never told me anything until just now, and I think only because someone named Eoghan indicated he could. Bradach takes his role as a Reaper seriously."

Death let out a breath and glanced at the floor. "Balladyn told me about you. I then made the decision to have Eoghan send Bradach to you."

"Knowing how much Bradach hates and distrusts the Dark?" Maeve would never have made such a move. Then again, Death had proven that she knew her Reapers well enough to put such a plan into motion.

Death grinned. "Bradach has a way of seeing things that others don't. He's also cool-headed. I knew if anyone could do this mission and succeed, it was him."

"You chose him as a Reaper wisely."

"I made a mistake that I've paid dearly for. It's one I swore never to make again."

Maeve's stomach dropped to her feet. This was where Death would kill her. No. If she were going to die, she would already be dead. Most likely, Death was going to tell her that she wasn't good enough for Bradach.

How could she argue with that? It wouldn't matter how much she loved him if Death didn't give them a chance. But then Maeve realized what it came down to. It was imperative that the identities of the Reapers remain secret.

The sadness that realization brought was so thick that it felt as if she were being slowly swallowed by quicksand. It felt worse than knowing that the Trackers and Usaeil would find her soon.

"I'm not going to punish Bradach," Death said. "He didn't find Xaneth as I'd hoped, but thanks to you, we were able to locate Usaeil and learn of the Trackers so we could prepare our next move."

Maeve didn't want to wait around to be dismissed. She quickly said, "I have no right to ask this, but I would like to fight beside you and the others standing against Usaeil. I don't ask because I fear the Trackers or dying. I ask because I'm good in battle. Not nearly as good as the Reapers, but I can hold my own. I know you have the Dragon Kings, Balladyn, and the Dark army, and I'm just one more person. But I want, no . . . I need to be a part of this."

"Because of Bradach?"

"Partly because of him, but also because it's the right thing to do."

Death regarded Maeve silently for a moment. "You were raised as a Dark. You've lived as a Dark. Yet you aren't fully one."

Maeve looked away and took in a steadying breath. "My father never asked me to become Dark. He loved me for who I am. He showed me nothing but love and gentleness. When I took over his business, I knew I'd have to embrace being Dark." Maeve snorted. "Oddly enough, in positions of power, there are always others willing to do the . . . dirty work."

"So, you never killed anyone."

"Only in self-defense. I've never murdered anyone or killed for pleasure."

"Thereby ensuring that your eyes never turned red."

Maeve wasn't sure if Death was pleased by that or not. It was impossible to tell what Death was thinking, and since Maeve had built her empire on reading people, she found herself in unfamiliar territory. Even Bradach had been easier to read than Death.

"Some might consider themselves Light just from that," Death added.

"No Light has silver in their hair."

"That's not entirely true."

Hope sprang up in Maeve, though she wasn't sure why. "I've never heard of such a Fae."

"Shara was once Dark. She's from a prominent Dark family, but she fell in love with a Dragon King."

Maeve frowned. "Are you saying that a Dark can become Light?"

"Why do you sound so surprised?" Death asked. "If it's so easy for a Light to become Dark, why shouldn't it be just as easy for a Dark to become Light?"

"Because of the evil a Dark does."

"It's not about the deeds so much as what's inside each individual. If you feed the darkness within you, then you'll be Dark."

"And if you feed the light, then a Fae will be Light," Maeve finished.

Death gave a nod of her black head. "Precisely. The fact of the matter is that you are neither one or the other. You are both. The best parts of both, I believe."

Maeve was taken aback by Death's words. She didn't know how to respond, so she didn't.

Death looked around at the ballroom. "You created an empire, and you did it with class. Were you merciless as they called you?" Lavender eyes slid back to Maeve. "Yes, but then rulers often have to be. I mentioned a mistake I made earlier. It nearly cost me everything. I'm cautious now."

"As you should be."

"Be that as it may, I've scrutinized you, Maeve. I've watched every move you've made over the last two days. I saw the lengths you went to in order to try and save Leon, I saw you fight valiantly beside my Reapers, and I saw you risk everything to stand with a Fae you barely know, simply because you wanted to."

It sounded as if Death were impressed, but Maeve wasn't about to get her hopes up. She prepared herself for the worst, just in case.

"Bradach mentioned that I no longer enforced my rule of no relationships. It was the right thing to do. However," she said, her lavender eyes glittering dangerously, "that doesn't mean I allow just anyone in. Every Reaper was betrayed and then killed. I'll not have another betrayal done to them."

Maeve nodded solemnly. "They're your family. You're looking out for them."

"They are my family, yes. We're a mix of Dark and Light Fae and . . . other."

Maeve knew the other Death referred to was herself. Because Maeve was under no illusions that the being she spoke with was a mere Fae. There was too much power, too much intensity in her.

Death cocked her head to the side. "You won't profess not to betray us?"

"I've learned that actions speak louder than words. Words are meaningless. If it takes a thousand years, I will prove to you and everyone else that I love Bradach and will never betray him, you, or any Reaper."

Death quirked a brow. "You would wait that long?"

"You need proof, and if that's what it takes, then I'll do it. I just ask that I be able to see Bradach. And I would still like to fight with you against Usaeil."

"Balladyn was right. You would make a good queen."

Maeve found herself shocked once more. "My king said that?"

"I spoke with him before I brought you here. He holds you in high regard. So does Aisling, Eoghan, and the others. And it goes without saying that Bradach does."

"And you?" It was pushing things for Maeve to ask such a question, but she needed to know.

Death suddenly smiled. "I like you. I also think you're a good match for Bradach. But I have to ask if you're with him simply because you think it will keep the Trackers and Usaeil from you."

Anger churned in Maeve. "I already told you that has nothing to do with it. I loved Bradach before I knew who he was. I'll face the next Tracker and the next and the next on my own. I want to be with Bradach because I love him. Not for any other reason."

"Are you sure you know what you're getting into? Being with a Reaper means that he will put you second—always."

"I don't need to be taken care of. I can look out for myself," Maeve replied.

"In order to be with Bradach, you'll have to leave the empire you've built behind. You would leave your wealth, your friends, all of it?"

Maeve laughed wryly as she glanced around her. "I have nothing and no one. My so-called empire is most likely already being picked to pieces. And I don't care. Whether you approve of me or not, I'll be walking away from all of this."

Death suddenly held out her hand. "My name is Erith."

Maeve looked at the outstretched hand before she took it. In the next instant, they were on a tiny isle in the middle of a lake. Erith released her hand and walked through a Fae doorway. Maeve hurried to follow and found herself in another world.

"This is my realm," Erith said proudly while gazing at the

white tower. "Or it was until recently. Now, all the Reapers and their lovers live here."

Maeve's gaze darted from one beautiful flower to another. There were so many trees and animals that she grew dizzy trying to look at all of them.

Then she remembered Bradach. Her head snapped to Death. "Is he here?"

Erith's smile was kind as she pointed to a distant mountain. "He was there the last time Eoghan found him. Or you can call to him."

"No," Maeve said with a shake of her head. "I want to go to him." Just before she teleported away, she took Death's hand in hers. "Thank you. You won't regret bringing me here. I'll never let Bradach or any of you down."

"I know," Death said with a grin.

Maeve saw a man approaching with black hair and deep purple eyes, but she was too excited about seeing Bradach to stay and meet him. She would introduce herself to the others later. First, Bradach.

She teleported to the mountaintop. But as she looked around, she saw no sign of Bradach. Maeve descended the mountain, keeping to the side that faced the white tower. For the next forty minutes, she worked her way from one side to the other before descending some more.

Then she saw him. Bradach sat cross-legged on an outcropping of rock that was half-hidden from view. She wanted to shout out to him in her euphoria, but she bit back her yell and continued her descent.

She stood behind him, her heart bursting with joy. The emotions were so thick that they welled within her, causing her eyes to burn with tears of happiness.

Suddenly, Bradach's head turned, and he saw her. He was on his feet in the next second with his arms around her. For long minutes, they simply held each other. No words were needed. Their love and contentment filled the silence.

"I'm yours. Always," she told him.

Bradach leaned back and placed his hands on either side of her face. "And I'm yours. I was from the moment I first saw you, and I'll be yours until the end of time."

"Together."

He gave her a tender kiss on the lips. "Forever."

Dubhan lowered his veil behind the Tracker and waited for the ugly fek to turn around. As soon as the creature did, Dubhan smiled. "Took you long enough."

The Tracker peeled back his lips to show his fangs.

"You're going to have to do better than that," he said to the beast. Dubhan sighed loudly when the Tracker formed a ball of magic in his hand. "I take that to mean you won't be telling me where Xaneth is."

The Tracker growled right before he threw the orb. Dubhan dodged the magic as he stalked to the creature. The Reapers needed one of them alive. This one would do nicely. Even though he'd much rather kill it. But he had orders.

Dubhan kicked the beast between his legs. He grinned when the Tracker grabbed his aching bits and fell to his knees. Dubhan wasted no time in punching the creature in the face to knock him out.

"Now, the fun begins," Dubhan said as he teleported the beast to the compound on Inchmickery off Scotland's east coast.

She was going to kill them all. Each and every Reaper. Usaeil would take great pleasure in ripping each of them apart. She would save Death for last. The torture she had in store for Death would eclipse anything she'd ever even imagined doing to her enemies.

Usaeil walked the corridors of her castle using glamour to disguise herself as Inen. Everyone was talking about her—and none of it was good. Her people had not only learned of her involvement with the humans, but they also had pictures.

Fury ran so hotly within Usaeil that she had to fight against lashing out at those around her.

It would feel so goooooooooood.

The darkness within her was hard to ignore, but she hadn't worked so hard for what she had only to lose it all simply because she couldn't hold in her anger. But there was one she could take it out on.

Usaeil quickly made her way to her private chambers and then used the Fae doorway to get to Xaneth. She stalked to him and sank her nails into his chest.

His back bowed as a scream of pain welled from him. Usaeil smiled. Soon, all her enemies would be wailing just like her nephew. It was all coming together beautifully.

Thank you for reading **DARK ALPHA'S REDEMPTION**.
I hope you enjoyed the story as much as I loved writing it.

If you want more Reapers, then you're in luck!
Up next is **DARK ALPHA'S TEMPTATION**.

BUY DARK ALPHA'S TEMPTATION NOW
at www.DonnaGrant.com

◆

And don't miss out on the Dark Kings series.
The next book set in Dark Universe, is **FEVER** …

BUY FEVER NOW
at www.DonnaGrant.com

◆

To find out when new books release
SIGN UP FOR MY NEWSLETTER today at
https://www.tinyurl.com/DonnaGrantNews

Join my Facebook group, Donna Grant Groupies, for exclusive
giveaways and sneak peeks of future books.
https://bit.ly/DGGroupies

◆

Keep reading for a peek of DARK ALPHA'S TEMPTATION and a
glimpse at FEVER …

SNEAK PEEK AT DARK ALPHA'S TEMPTATION

REAPER SERIES, BOOK 9

Some temptations are worth the fall.

I am a Reaper—an elite assassin bound to Death. Obedience is all I've ever known.

I carry out the command without hesitation, without mercy, without question.

Until Kyra.

She is fire and defiance, all sharp edges and unbreakable will. The moment she steps into my world, the darkness loosens its grip—and that terrifies me more than any enemy ever has. She makes me want. She makes me feel. She makes me question the one thing I was never meant to doubt.

The answers we need are buried in her past.

But the closer I get, the harder it is to remember she was ever meant to be just a mission.

Kyra doesn't simply tempt me—she unravels me.

Every touch threatens my control.

Every look dares me to choose her over duty.

And with each breath, I feel myself slipping further from the Reaper I was forged to be.

Defying Death means facing consequences that span time itself.

But losing Kyra would destroy what little remains of me.

If temptation is my downfall, so be it.

I'll challenge the past. And I'll fight for the future.

New York Times* and *USA Today* bestselling author Donna Grant delivers a fiercely sensual tale of forbidden desire, dangerous choices, and a Reaper willing to defy fate itself.

BUY DARK ALPHA'S TEMPTATION TODAY

at www.DonnaGrant.com

Excerpt

Drumshanbo, Ireland
June

It was good to be right.

Then again, Kyra was always right. The pub was more crowded than usual, but she paid the patrons no attention as she tossed back the whisky and quietly set the empty glass on the bar before weaving her way through the people to the side door.

Her target didn't see her. Though she made a point of not being seen. It was a gift her aunt had taught her, and Kyra put the skill to good use. Still, she never imagined she'd use her talent to follow a Reaper.

She slipped out of the pub into the summer night. Drumshanbo might be a small village, but it was a mecca for travelers since it was perfectly situated and contained woodlands, rolling hills, and lakes, as well as the Iron Mountains.

The Reaper halted. Kyra ducked into a nearby alley and waited several seconds before she walked out as if she hadn't been following him. The Reaper was gone. This wasn't the first time she'd lost him, but she wasn't rattled by it at all.

Kyra sensed that she was being watched. No doubt by the Reaper himself. She inwardly smiled and walked to her motorbike. She strapped on her helmet and then put on her gloves before starting the engine. Something had brought the Reaper to Drumshanbo, and she was going to find out what it was.

She revved the engine before checking her blind spot and pulling out into traffic. It wasn't long before Kyra was out of the village and on the dark, winding roads. She pointed her motorbike toward the mountains. The cabin she'd chosen was out of the way, which meant that there was no reason for anyone to drive past it.

The truth was that she liked being at the top of the ridge. She enjoyed the view, but really, she liked that it reminded her of the stories her aunt used to tell her about the Fae Realm and all its wonders.

Kyra parked the bike next to the cottage and walked to the door. She paused, putting her hand against the edge of the door to feel for the wards she'd placed. They hadn't been disturbed. Her magic wasn't exceptionally strong, but she was able to do a multitude of things that other Fae couldn't. Besides, it didn't matter how strong her magic was because she doubted there would be anything that could keep a Reaper out if he wanted in badly enough.

She gave a little push with her magic, and the door opened, undoing both the human and the Fae locks. She set her helmet, gloves, and keys on the small table inside the door before she removed her jacket and raked her fingers through her hair. There was a bump against her leg before a meow reached her. Kyra leaned down and scratched the cat behind the ears. The tiny calico had shown up the first day Kyra arrived, and the animal had been coming around ever since. Kyra had no idea how the cat kept getting inside, but in truth, it was nice to return and find the animal there. Not that the cat stayed. Just long enough to eat, maybe get in a little nap, and then the calico was gone until the next day.

"Did you have a good day?" Kyra asked as she picked up the cat and walked into the kitchen.

The cat purred loudly, rubbing its head against Kyra's chin. She laughed as she got the can of cat food out of the cabinet. The cat jumped out of her arms and wound around Kyra's legs as she dished out the meal.

She set the dish down and squatted beside the animal as it began eating. "In case you were wondering, I had a pretty good day myself. I saw him again. I'm going to need to be more careful, though. I don't wish to anger him before I've had a chance to speak to him."

The cat looked up, blinking its big, green eyes at her.

Kyra twisted her lips. "You should see him. He's . . . well, let's just say he turns heads."

The cat licked her muzzle and simply stared.

Kyra rolled her eyes and straightened. "Fine. He's mouthwateringly gorgeous. Is that what you want me to say?"

In answer, the calico went back to eating.

Kyra sighed and walked to the desk. She spread out the pictures she'd taken of the Reaper. She didn't need the human contraption to remember his face, but she liked being able to stare at the photos of him. She wished she knew his name. He was tall and broad-shouldered and walked with a confidence that caused others to give him a wide berth. He used glamour to shield his eyes and hair around humans, but she had gotten to see his true coloring.

Deep crimson eyes that showed not an ounce of mercy. Black hair with silver weaved throughout the thick length that was longer on top and shorter on the sides.

She should be wary of him. Not only was he a Reaper, but he was also Dark. Those two things should've been all she needed to steer clear. Instead, she had found herself enraptured. Completely smitten.

Utterly infatuated.

It had been by pure accident that she'd even discovered there were Reapers. And if the seven of them—along with the one Dark female—hadn't been fighting a dozen pale-skinned creatures at the Light Castle, they would've noticed her. Thankfully, their attention had been on the beasts, which allowed her a view of the battle, something she'd likely never see again.

Kyra knew the face of all seven Reapers, but it was the one she followed that stood out to her. It had nothing to do with his kissable lips, penetrating eyes, or his amazing body. That was a lie she couldn't even tell herself. There had been something about the Reaper's face that had pulled at Kyra instantly.

Perhaps she would've had better luck following the female Dark with her long braids and red nails.

Kyra shook her head. The moment her eyes had landed on her Reaper, she hadn't been able to look away. He had fought like a wild man. He was savage and ferocious, and she hadn't been able to look at anyone or anything else. He hadn't given any quarter to the beasts. And Kyra had a feeling that her Reaper looked at the world just like that.

No quarter.

No forgiveness.

Her gaze ran over the face in the photo. Hollow cheeks, thin lips, regal nose, and a square jawline. It was a face she would never forget. It was also one she would never share with anyone else.

The Fae, in general, were terrified of the Reapers. Some didn't believe the Reapers were real, while others were wholeheartedly convinced of them. Like all Fae children, Kyra had been told the stories as a kid. She'd feared the Reapers for much of her life, but after a while, when she'd found no proof of them, that terror began to ebb.

It wasn't until the battle at the Light Castle that she realized the Reapers were real. Well, to be fair, she hadn't known who the seven warriors were at first, but it didn't take her long to piece it together.

The Dark female that battled with them? Well, that was another piece of the puzzle Kyra hadn't figured out yet. She would eventually, but right now, her attention was on her Reaper and finding out everything she could about him.

It was dangerous. She knew that, but there wasn't much about her life that wasn't. She'd been living on the fringes of the Fae world for centuries now, interacting with both sides and gaining information she could pass on. Most times, she dealt more with the humans, but she still made sure to get to the Light Castle often to keep up with what was going on with the Fae.

The castle was a hub of information for the Light. All Kyra had to do was hang out there for a few hours, and she was able to learn all kinds of juicy gossip. Most of it was nonsense, but she always came away with a gem or two.

She set the photo down and leaned back in the chair to prop her feet up on the edge of the desk. Her mother had wanted her to be a proper lady. It was expected of any female in their family line, but Kyra had rebelled. She'd wanted to go her own way. Her father had humored her, but her mother had fought her on every little thing until Kyra couldn't take it anymore.

That's when her aunt stepped in. Eva had gone through something very similar to Kyra, so her aunt had decided to take matters into her own hands. It was Eva who made sure that Kyra kept a relationship with her parents. It was also Eva who'd taught her how to embrace what made her different, but also to accept and love what made her part of their family.

Kyra missed Eva deeply. Her aunt had gone missing over a century ago. It wasn't like Eva at all, which is why Kyra had known that something was wrong. But no matter where she looked, no matter who she asked, no one had any answers. It was like Eva had just stopped existing one day.

There were answers, and Kyra was going to find them. There was a chance that the Reapers might know something. It was a long shot, but at this point, Kyra was reaching for anything. If only she could learn more about the Reapers before she approached them. There was very little to go on, though, and even less that anyone knew.

She had asked around and got a different answer about the Reapers from nearly everyone she spoke with. No one seemed to know anything for sure. And since she was the only Light who had somehow managed to see the battle with the creatures, no one knew what she was talking about.

Kyra dropped her feet to the floor and rose. She walked to the bathroom and stared at her reflection. She ran her fingers through her long hair, using magic to shift the green locks to a light pink. As a final touch, she changed the length, altering it to chin-length with the right side shaved.

No matter what hairstyle or color she tried, she had yet to find anything she kept for more than a day. It also prevented others from recognizing her, which was a big help when she was trailing a Reaper who had keen senses.

She really wished she knew his name.

More than that, she wanted to know what it was about him that drew her.

"A Dark and a Reaper." Kyra shook her head at her reflection. "Yeah. That's real smart. Eva would kick your ass into next month for being so dumb."

The smile died as her mind drifted once more to her aunt. Kyra pushed away from the sink and walked outside to stand beneath the night sky. There was something calming about looking at the stars. She stayed there for a long time, thinking of the past and the path she found herself on now. She hoped the Reapers had resources she didn't to locate Eve, because she was willing to do whatever was necessary to find her family.

With a sigh, Kyra went back inside to the bedroom. She removed her boots and clothes and slipped into a short gown made of white silk. Then she lay on the bed. She gazed up at the ceiling, her mind going over everything from that day. Her Reaper had seemed to be searching for something. Or someone. He didn't talk to anyone, just walked the streets and occasionally went into a pub, though he never stayed long.

She could have lost his trail at any time. So far, he'd been relatively easy to find, going from one village to the next. But how long would that last? Maybe it was time that she approached him. What harm would it do to talk to him?

She scrunched up her face at the thought. It was probably the worst idea she'd ever had. Only second to the one where she'd decided to follow him in the first place.

Kyra had seen him fight. She knew exactly what he was capable of and how quickly he moved. No doubt he had other skills she didn't know about. That had led her to wonder how long she could follow him without him knowing. She was good, but he was a Reaper.

Kyra blew out a breath. The best thing would be for her to forget her Reaper. To let him go his way as she went another. Yeah. That would be the smart thing to do.

But she wouldn't.

She knew it with the same certainty that she knew she would never own a pair of high heels. There were just some things that weren't her—and giving up was one of them.

Though her real motivation for trailing her Reaper was to get answers, that wasn't all of it. In fact, she was pretty sure she was following him simply because she couldn't stop following him.

"Oh, Mum would just love hearing that," she told herself with a roll of her eyes.

If only she could find a reliable source to tell her more about the Reapers. She wanted details. All the details. Especially about one Dark Reaper with large hands and broad shoulders and red eyes she couldn't stop thinking about.

She closed her eyes as her body pulsed with desire, a need that went soul-deep. It was the same each time she thought about him. It had happened the first time she saw him, as well. Like some switch had been flipped the moment her gaze landed on him.

Almost as if she had . . . come alive . . . at the sight of him. All she thought about was him. And her dreams? The things he did to her in her fantasies made her tremble with need.

Kyra rolled onto her side and tried to ignore her body, but she knew it was useless. There would be no sleep until she gave herself some relief. The hunger would be back in the morning, but at least she would have a few hours of respite.

She flopped onto her back and let thoughts of her Reaper fill her mind as her hand drifted between her legs.

BUY DARK ALPHA'S TEMPTATION NOW
at www.DonnaGrant.com

to fall into the arms of a Dragon King. But how can she resist Kelton when he's so willing to share his secrets and bear his soul? He hasn't met a beautiful, trustworthy woman like Bernadette in... forever. But once they give into their mutual desire, their worlds will never be the same. Soon Bernadette must face her dilemma: Should she expose the truth about Kelton in the name of science? Or join him in his battle with the dark forces—in the name of love?

BUY FEVER TODAY
at www.DonnaGrant.com

ABOUT THE AUTHOR

New York Times and *USA Today* bestselling author Donna Grant® has been praised for her "totally addictive" and "unique and sensual" stories.

She's written more than one hundred novels spanning multiple genres of romance including the bestselling Dragon Kings® series that features a thrilling combination of Druids, Fae, and immortal Highlanders who are dark, dangerous, and irresistible. She lives in Texas with her dog and a cat.

www.DonnaGrant.com
www.MotherofDragonsBooks.com

facebook.com/AuthorDonnaGrant
instagram.com/dgauthor
tiktok.com/@donnagrant_author
bookbub.com/authors/donna-grant
goodreads.com/donna_grant
pinterest.com/donnagrant1

* 9 7 8 1 9 5 8 3 5 3 8 5 1 *